Joseph Cox's

The Barn

And other Torah Stories

Volume 5:
Deuteronomy - דברים

Joseph J. Cox

Published by Big Picture Books

Modiin, Israel

Cover Photography from Shutterstock

Edited by Wouter Dreyer

Feedback from many friends & associates – you know who you are!

Dedicated to my children

The life of our people continues with them

Contents

Introduction

The idea of using stories to explain moral concepts is probably as old as human vocabulary itself. Stories, not rules or arguments, have generational impact, transferring values from one generation to the next. They establish and explain the core character of the societies that carry them. Because of this power, stories have long been used to explain concepts in the Torah.

However, to modern ears many such stories are foreign; either their concepts are unfamiliar, or their styles fail to grip the modern conscious.

This book provides a new set of modern, relatable and engaging stories. They cross many genres and are meant to engage many different kinds of people. I know that writing them has left me with a far stronger understanding of the Torah, of humanity and of the world that surrounds us.

Perhaps you, the reader, can find that same understanding. And, perhaps, these stories will also strengthen your relationship to G-d and your understanding of our place in the world.

Thank you,

Joseph Cox

Echoes

The following story focuses on themes that run throughout the book of Devarim (Deuteronomy).

Anna

I sense it then. In a sudden mad burst, I sense it. The words float in my head, not quite there – but there, on the edge of my awareness. If I look at them, I know they will flee. If I do not, I know they will persevere – demanding reality, driving at my consciousness even as I cannot quite wrap my head around them.

All is dark. All but the words that are there and not yet there at all.

I sense them, on the edge. They are cast up in shapes of razor wire and silk and wood and wool. They wrap around each other, curling into a shape that defies beginning and end. I sense them. I know they are there. I know I must capture what is before me.

A moment passes, the shapes enfold *me*, wrapping around *me*.

After just a moment, they disappear.

I open my eyes and I'm back in my apartment.

All around me I see the words. The words of previous visions. Strands of metal and glue and bits of shattered glass enameled together. Some are words encased in cubes of semi-translucent plastic. Some dangle from the ceilings, open and unencumbered. Each one has a story. Each one came with a vision. I felt each poem, sensed it, before I gave it reality.

Each one pummeled me, demanding that I give it life.

I could do nothing else until that mission was complete.

I see my life in this room. I see beauty. I see G-d.

And this poem.... this poem is no different.

I glance to my workbench. Materials are there, they are everywhere really. Scraps I've collected in case I might need them. But something is missing. I see a bit of metal in my mind, but not on the desk. It is gold colored, but not gold. A copper wire, perhaps?

Yes, I realize. That is it.

I stand and rush towards the door, my eyes already roving in search of my prey.

I have no choice.

Until I capture the poem in reality, until I give it life, I will be pursued by it.

I must make it real.

The poems used to be rare. My parents were so worried when I was a little girl. I had seizures, that's what they called them. But even when I was little, I saw them as epiphanies. I would rush afterwards, as if commanded by some force, to make what I had seen real. Somehow my parents didn't immediately connect the two events. I produced art, strange art, powerful art. They couldn't understand where it had come from. I told them about the seizures, but they didn't think I was having epiphanies. I had MRIs as the doctors tried to catch me in the act, as they tried to figure out what was wrong with me.

Eventually, they settled on a cocktail of anti-seizure and anti-psychotic drugs. They couldn't figure out which was more critical. I still felt the visions although they were somehow muted. They lacked definition. They cried out to me – for me to make them real. But I could not. Because I could not begin to grasp them.

My parents were pleased, the doctors were pleased. A dose of anti-depressants were added to my daily quantity of pills. And then everybody seemed pleased. But I was not pleased. The poems were still calling to me. Quietly. I felt their distance like a loss. I mourned them as others celebrated their absence.

I knew my mission though. I poured myself into art at school. I overheard my parents speaking of their pride in me. I had such skill, such promise. They understood, on some level, that my tortured mind was behind my talent. But they still hoped that I could thread a path to greatness, without insanity.

I didn't share their hope.

For me insanity and greatness were one and the same.

When I turned 18, I ran from my home. I didn't want the medications any more. There was little my parents could do. The age of asylums had passed. Eventually, I found myself in another city. Then in a city-run shelter. Then in a subsidized apartment. I tried to hold down a job. But when my seizures came, in all their glorious reality, I would lose whatever job I had.

I would just walk away, or run, seeking what I needed to bring reality to my living dreams.

I am not working now. I am under the power of that same force. I rush out of my apartment and down to the street. The sun bursts against my eyes. The sound of traffic from the four-lane thoroughfare outside my building assaults me. I stagger, but just for a moment. Then I lift my arm, cover my face against the sun, and begin my mad rush down the street. I ignore the noise of the road.

The neighborhood is not a good one, but the people know me. They know I have nothing worth stealing. And they know, from the crazy glint in my eye, that it would be dangerous to slow my progress. We are troubled, all of us. Yet we live more than most.

I run down the sidewalk, seeking the golden glint of my dreams.

I need it to make the poem real.

I need it to make the ball of truth wrap around the emptiness of humanity.

I need it.

And then I see it. My sight seems to focus on it, lasering in like some tactical computer in a movie. There is an old computer monitor, lying on the sidewalk, on the other side of the thoroughfare. It will have the wire I need.

I know it is all I need to make the poem real.

I rush straight towards it.

Others might say that I saw the cars too late to avoid them. But it would not be true. I saw them, but I had no choice but to go.

I needed to make the poem real.

The Cleaner

My boss hands me a clipboard. It has a list of addresses, last occupants and new addresses for those people. The list is of city apartments recently vacated by their occupants. My job is to clean them. This isn't a dainty job; there's a lot more hauling than scrubbing.

Most of the spaces for new addresses simply have the word "unknown" filled in. The occupants have simply disappeared. But not all have. A few have found new homes. Somebody has filled in those addresses, although I don't know why. It's not like we do anything with the information. "Unknown" is not the only time our trail runs cold. Some days the word "deceased" marks the end of an occupant's residential history.

There is one such entry today. A woman named "Anna Stokes."

"She was hit by a car," my boss volunteers.

I nod. I'd actually seen her die. I'd been taking a break just then, looking out the window of an apartment my crew had been cleaning. I'd seen the woman running madly down the sidewalk and then dash into traffic. Psychotic woman. She probably hadn't been taking her meds.

The whole neighborhood is psychotic.

But hey, it pays my bills.

When I'm done reviewing the list, I tuck the clipboard under my arm, gather my crew, and head out.

There are four of us. We have a truck and a chute for lower-level apartments. The job is simple. We get to crawl through the muck of the mentally disturbed and addicted dregs of society. And we get to throw out that muck; like we're cleaning out the bottom of a hamster's cage. Any society needs to dispose of its detritus.

Just like you would do when you clean a hamster's cage, we isolate ourselves from our work. Depending on the apartment, we have a wide variety of safety equipment at our disposal, from full hazmat suits to simple needle-safe gloves. I tend to err on the side of caution. These people have (or had, case depending) a lot of issues.

The work isn't awesome. But we're City employees. We get paid union wages and union benefits in return for our efforts. I am curious sometimes though. Morbidly curious. Just how bad can an apartment get? What kind of situation does the kind of whack job who runs into traffic leave behind?

I'm thinking about that when I choose our first job for the day. I decide that we'll start with Anna Stokes.

When we get to her apartment, we open the door, slowly. Our masks in our hands and ready for our faces. We're used to some pretty awful – and sometimes dangerous – odors. But there's nothing. There's no smell of rotting food or human waste. There's just a slight odor of rust and maybe glue.

We let the masks fall to our sides and then pull the door open the rest of the way. As I look around the apartment, I see the paint is peeling and everything is in disrepair. That's expected. I wouldn't maintain a city apartment. Something else is strange, though. Very strange. A tangled mass of metal and glass and who knows what else seems to fill the entirety of the space between the walls, the floor and the ceiling. You can barely walk through the crap this woman left behind.

As we look at it, we know that it will take all day to clean.

But... union wages and union benefits.

We'll be okay.

We don gloves and set to work, bagging object after object in our extra thick plastic bags. I notice that some of the shapes seem to contain something resembling letters, words and even sentences. They are laid out in screwed-up patterns, their media forced into some unnatural configuration.

The woman was clearly insane.

I pick up one of the objects. It is a small sphere. It fits in my hand. The outside is a roughly formed mirror, but not quite. I can just make out shapes within it. I stare at it and see there is a word in there, but I can't tell what it is. I don't know why, but I stick that little sphere in my own bag.

I'll take it home.

Maybe I'll show it to my dog.

It takes all day to finish the job. We leave the apartment empty and drive our truck full of reinforced plastic bags straight to the dump. That's all there is.

Another mess of a life disposed of. Everything gone.

Nothing worth saving. Probably not even that little sphere.

I get home, put the sphere on my little kitchen table, and do what I always do: Grab a beer and some leftovers. Watch a game. Pet the dog. Go to sleep.

I don't sleep well, though. The sphere is in my dreams. I'm looking at it, trying to see what is inside. But all I can see is myself. I turn it in my hands. I stare at it.

I try, somehow, to get through that strange outer skin.

But all I can see is myself.

I wake up suddenly, my body covered in sweat.

For a second, I don't know where I am. And then I notice the clock. 3:05 AM.

I get out of bed and make my way to the kitchen. The sphere is there, sitting on the kitchen table. I pick it up, almost like I'm programmed to do exactly that. Somehow, it seems more opaque than it had the day before. I hold it up to the light, but I still can't make out what lays on the inside.

Eventually, I go back to sleep. The sphere is still there, hiding its inner self from me.

I keep working, in the days and weeks that follow. But the sphere becomes an obsession. I need to know what it contains. It is an irrational drive, but I can't seem to stop it. I consider destroying the outer shell, but the thought repulses me almost as soon as I conceive of it.

I spend my off hours turning the little object in my hands. Gradually, I realize just how beautifully it is constructed. It is not simply a glass ball, but a ball made of pieces of glass fused together to create something I know is entirely intentional. There is nothing sloppy about it.

Whatever it is, the woman who made it put both heart and skill into its reality.

As the weeks pass, I begin to understand that the thing is precious. Even magical.

I begin to understand that I have it for a reason.

One day, I'm cleaning out the apartment of a man who overdosed on Fentanyl when I see his diary. I pick it up in my gloved hands. And I open it. I see the man's pain pouring out of the pages.

I take it.

I take his diary and put it in my bag. I don't know why. I never used to save anything.

When I get home, I open the diary. I read it from cover to cover. I learn what drove the man to drugs long before the drugs drove him to death. I spend hours reading his story.

When I finally close the little book and look up at the sphere, it has changed.

Just a bit of it has somehow clarified.

I can make out a single letter inside. It is a 'T'.

I feel a sudden regret that I destroyed all the other objects in Anna Stokes' apartment. I realize now that I'd stuffed treasures into those thick plastic bags, never to be seen again.

That night, I dream of the sphere again. It is the same dream. But it doesn't torture me in the same way.

The next day, the next job, I steal a trinket from a woman's house. It is a knot of metal, worried into shape by the unceasing hands of a meth addict.

I steal again. And again.

My apartment begins to fill with the leftovers of tragic lives. I mail some of it away, to the addresses listed on the job sheet. But most of it has no place to go. So, I keep it.

With those little objects I see, somehow, into the lives of those who have gone.

Strangest of all, the sphere begins to open to me. After months have passed, I find myself able to see past my own distorted image.

There is a word inside, written in stone so finely carved that it looks like bone.

The word is 'TRUTH.'

I keep collecting the leftovers of lives lost. Eventually, they outgrow my apartment. I rent another space and it becomes a gallery of sorts. I invite others to visit; to learn about the lives of those who struggled.

The gallery grows. Others bring what they have collected. Soon it is a museum. Volunteers begin to care for it and all that it contains. It lives on the charity of others.

I still clean for the City. But it has become far more than a good union job with good union benefits.

It has become a sacred calling.

Much of the book of Devarim (Deuteronomy) is about the creation of a society-wide consciousness. Like Pinocchio, the nation as a whole seems to come to life. Even as it does so, it remains an amalgamation of individuals. Ideally, this is our reality. We are individuals, with our own lives. But we are also a part of a far greater life – a life beyond our own.

Much as we might try, we can't consciously control our impact on our societies. We can't choose what others take from our lives and make a part of their own. Anna Stokes created many things, but only one survived. And she could not choose which one that was. It simply had to catch the fancy of a City employed cleaner.

Despite this limit, the echo of that creation reverberated far beyond her. A small part of her voice was taken up by the cleaner and amplified far more than it could ever have been within the confines of her own little world.

A little more than three months have passed since my mother's death. One of her last actions was to make me responsible for her intellectual property; for her writing. Even as I seek to share her work, I know the library I am responsible for is only a small fraction of what she had to give. Of all her decades of study and thought and knowledge, only a tiny snippet will survive. It will survive in her students or it will survive in those who read one of her books. It will survive not because she wanted it to, but because those who heard or read her words were impacted by them.

Once we speak, we can no longer control how our words are used.

It might seem terribly sad, and on an individual level, it is. So much is lost. But like Anna Stokes' work, her work – and my work, and your work – can all have a life beyond our own.

Near the very end of the Book of Devarim, there is a poem. It is almost impossible for us to penetrate its meaning. When we read it, we often see our own reflections in it. But the poem is described as a witness against us. It stands, like that sphere, testifying to who we can be.

It testifies to truth by reminding us of our own failures; and of what we do not choose to see.

Beyond the details, I believe there is a more general reality. Like the cleaner in the story, we have to allow the Torah to penetrate us. We have to allow it to disturb us. We have to allow it to drive us to see possibilities we would otherwise ignore.

Because, in the final rendering of things, it is only when we open our eyes to a truth beyond ourselves that we can see past our own reflections. It is only then that we can be a part of reality of Torah.

It is only then that our people can truly come to life.

Devarim: Coming of Age

Moses Hassan looked around as he walked slowly to the dais at the west end of the room. There was a good crowd here, nearly three hundred people.

Moses wondered what the guests had thought of the party so far. Moses counted the rich and powerful of the City among his friends. When those friends had Bar Mitzvahs or weddings, they rented hotels or dedicated halls. This space was nothing like that. To get here, the guests had had to walk through a gap in a fence – and on to a construction site. They had to don work helmets, safety shoes and protective glasses. And then they had to ride construction elevators – strapped to the sides of a still-rising skyscraper. The reception itself took place thirty floors up, in a newly-windowed double-story space that was far from complete. There was just unfinished concrete, construction lamps, and the day's remaining sunlight peering through the floor-to-ceiling windows on the western side of the building.

The room was done up well. There were round tables, tablecloths, fancy table settings, and even fabric covered chairs. It was obvious, despite the locale, that no expense had been spared. In this way, the setup was conventional. Moses was sure of it.

While he didn't know much about table settings, he knew how to hire experts.

Of course, the oddest thing about the affair wasn't the room or the tables. It was the guests.

While about half were indeed drawn from the City's rich and powerful, there were others there. There were crane operators, bookkeepers, plumbers, electricians and masons. There were city clerks and firefighters and even a few police officers. These people were dressed in their best clothes. For some that meant suits and ties. But for others, it was a clean pair of jeans and a white shirt. They were all mixed together. They were all honored guests at the Bar Mitzvah of Jonathan Hassan.

As Moses Hassan looked around the room, he saw the different groups eyeing each other, all of them more than a little uncomfortable among unusual neighbors.

Moses smiled, inwardly. After all, everything was happening exactly as he had intended it to.

When it came time to speak, Moses had considered just standing on a milk crate. But a milk crate would have taken away from the backdrop; the sun setting behind the tall buildings of the City itself. So, he had assembled a group of concrete bricks and then plastered over them, creating something that seemed to fit with the room as a whole.

Moses stepped up on to this rough dais, and then turned towards the room. He had practiced this speech so many times. The way he figured it, he had one son and that son had one Bar Mitzvah.

This was the most important talk he would ever give.

Moses had no notes. Instead, he just stood there and waited for the crowd to quiet. Voices settled, forks and knives were set down. The last surreptitious drinks were had. Then, there was silence.

Moses began to speak.

"Ten years ago, my time with Jonathan began. I didn't know it and he didn't know it. But it was true, nonetheless. Ten years ago, my wife, Shoshana Hassan, was diagnosed with breast cancer. I know many people in this room knew Shoshana. She is the reason I know you. In those days, I was building small multi-unit apartment buildings. I busied myself with contracts and with engineering and with project management. I felt good about what I was doing.

"But Shoshana understood there was more to life than making a bit of money on a few buildings. She got me to think about relationships – to value them and to invest in them and to be rewarded by them. I am so pleased to have all of you here. And that is because of her. All my success, my real success – my community success – is because of her.

"Ten years ago, Shoshana was diagnosed with breast cancer. We sought out the best doctors we could and they recommended that she undergo a radical and aggressive chemotherapy treatment. It was to begin immediately. She went into treatment without reservations. It is incredibly difficult to undergo this sort of therapy – it damn near kills even those who survive it. Since then, doctors have realized it isn't the best approach. But we acted on the information we had and Shoshana stayed the course without wavering. She did it so she could continue to make more of my world, and of yours.

"The doctors mentioned doing a procedure so we could have children after the chemotherapy. It wasn't the biggest of our concerns. And, we didn't have time for anything extra. I just needed Shoshana to survive. She gave my life meaning. I'm sure all of you who knew her can understand that.

"Six months after treatment started, it seemed like the chemotherapy had worked. She was coming out the other end. She was weak, certainly. Once again, we could think about the future. And we did. It was then that we truly understood she could never have children. I regretted my shortsightedness. How could we not have taken the few extra days needed before she started her chemotherapy?

"I thought I'd never overcome that regret. But I have since learned better."

Moses stopped, then took a deep and slow breath. A tremor in his voice, he continued.

"Shoshana was stronger than I was. She told me that we had so much to give, and so much to be thankful for. She told me we had to adopt a child. Not just any child though, a child who *needed* us. So, we started filling out the paperwork. We started looking and analyzing the options. Did we want a child from the US? Did we want a child from overseas? What did the different options involve? What kind of difficulties would we face?

"We only *started* that process, though.

"Just a few months after the chemo ended, Shoshana got sick again. The prognosis was as bad as it could be. We did nothing, we could do nothing. Shoshana lived a few weeks longer and then she left us.

"I buried my beloved wife. I was desperate for a time. But I *knew* what she had wanted. She had made that clear. In some kind of act of mourning, I decided *I* would adopt, and *I* would raise the child she would never meet. *I* filed out the forms, the agencies looked at *my* home. *I* went through the training. *I* passed through the steps *I* needed to pass through. Then, they handed me a catalog. They had some fancy name for it. But it was a catalog. They had pictures of different children and a little background on each one. The idea was that I would sit with a caseworker and I would order up one of the kids.

"I was blown away. How could I choose a child from a catalog? I started flipping through the pages. My heart grew sadder with each page. There were so many kids who couldn't be mine. There were so many I could help, but I could only choose one.

"And then I saw you, Jonathan. You were a gorgeous little kid. You had curly hair and beautiful features. But your eyes were tortured. You were four years old, but your eyes were full of pain. And I knew, just then, that *you* were the child I had to adopt. Then I looked at your brief little bio and one word popped out: 'cystic fibrosis.'"

"The case worker talked me through the challenges I would face. She took me through your history. Your mother and father had divorced less than a year after you were born. Your father just left. Your mother gave you up for adoption when you were three. She couldn't deal with the burden of *you* anymore.

"I met you a week after I found you in the catalog. We visited for a few months. Then, you became my son.

"Jonathan, you weren't an easy boy. You lived in a world over which you had no control. You had been abandoned and you were sick. The fact that *I* wanted you was irrelevant. Another reality had been baked into you and it was not so easy to escape it. But you showed, even from those early days, an almost instinctive touch of judgment. It was a simple thing. You were rigorous about using your PEP device. For those who don't know, a PEP is a face mask that creates pressure and enables Jonathan to clear his lungs. As I saw it, the use of that machine signaled the first step in who you would become.

"It was only a first step, though. In reality, the only control you could feel was the power to disrupt everything around you. You would throw incredible tantrums – especially considering you had such difficulty even breathing. It was, in its way, very impressive. You would sabotage anything you could – things, people, relationships. I tried to cut away at this reality. I tried to make you feel loved. But it wasn't easy. There is no formula for dealing with that sort of pain. Good outcomes aren't inevitable.

"When you grew a bit more, things got worse. You learned a new talent. You learned to blame everything on everybody but yourself. You couldn't do this or that because *I* had been unfair, or because your mother had been unfair. Or because G-d had been unfair. Nothing was up to you. You were incapable, as far as you saw it, of standing up to the difficulties of the world. And standing up wasn't, as you saw it, *your* responsibility.

"But, as everybody here knows, your story didn't stop there. *Our* story started with my love. My love of my wife and my love of a photograph in a catalog. I don't know how it happened, but you took this love and took chaos and despair and self-destruction and you began to form a cohesive person of yourself. You began to realize who you were.

"You didn't act on this awareness, not yet. You weren't engaging with the world, but just settling for what you did have. You were avoiding *doing*. You were satisfied with *being*. It was a big step up, but not enough to push you forward.

I came to you one day and told you, 'It is time do something.' You asked 'what?' I said that I didn't know, but I wasn't raising you *just* to live.

"We talked then. You came up with an idea. You decided you wanted to start a foundation. Its job would be simple: it would provide medical devices for children with genetic defects in the developing world. The PEP machine was key to your life. But cystic fibrosis isn't common in those places – it is primarily a Northern European disease. However, there are other devices that children with other conditions need. We started talking and planning and taking our very first steps towards realizing this project. I was excited about the possibilities.

"In the middle of this, when you were ten years-old, you asked to meet your birth parents. I thought it was a bad idea. You argued otherwise. Your entire childhood, you said, they had been holding you back. Their decision to abandon you had been holding you back. I agreed to the meeting. Your parents weren't dangerous people so you went to their homes and you talked to them, one on one. And then you came back to me and I could see, right away, that you had been right. A weight had been lifted from you.

"I asked you what had happened and your answer was simple. You realized, when you met them, that you were already bigger, better and more important than the limitations that had held your parents back. You were free of their decision. You were only 10 years old and you had overcome a challenge many can never overcome. But you didn't stop there.

"Jonathan, you have amazed me. You aren't like most kids. You have had to face overwhelming daily obstacles. You have to face, daily, fundamental threats to your own mortality. But despite all that, you kept going. We, together, hired a foundation manager. We actually visited Africa, not a safe trip for a kid with cystic fibrosis. We did it more than once, bringing a lot of equipment along the way. It cost a great deal. But *you* did it because you wanted to talk to the kids and the parents. You did it because you wanted to build relationships. You understand, in a way most don't, what really survives.

"As you know, Jonathan, we can't measure relationships. We can't see the ripples they create. But as my wife taught me, they are all that is real. You, Jonathan, a thirteen-year-old boy, already know what I did not understand as a fully-grown man.

"Today, you are becoming a young man. Unlike many young men, I've never had to tell you when another child is a bad influence. You have worked it out by yourself. You have learned to lock out those who are incompatible with the reality you are trying to create and you know there is no profit in *some* relationships. It takes strength to act against your own nature – your desire to reach out – but you are able to judge, despite your age, when that is for the best. I used to say that if my mind was too open, my brain would fall out. Jonathan, you understand that if your heart is too open, your reality will disappear.

"You don't stop there, though. That little hint of self-control – the use of the machine to clear your lungs – has only grown with time. Every night, before you go to sleep, you review your day. You keep a diary, like many others have done. But you do more than just that. You judge your own actions. You actively and consciously improve yourself. Even at your young age, you have focused yourself with a power that even I, a fully grown adult, am in awe of.

"But, my dear child, you still aren't where you need to be. And that is why I have brought all of these people here today. Jonathan, these people come from all walks of society. There are the rich and powerful, the aristocracy of New York. And there are masons and tradesmen and civil servants. I didn't invite them as some gesture towards social justice. I invited them, to this place, because I want you to connect to them, to relate to them. And to enable them to empower you. And to enable you to empower them."

Moses pauses and gestures broadly towards the darkening skyline behind him.

"Jonathan, this building, the one we are dining in, was built by the tradesmen in this room. It was financed by the bankers in this room. It has been protected by the policemen and the firemen. It has been reviewed and approved and improved by the civil servants. We work together. Certainly, we push and shove sometimes. But, fundamentally, we respect the place of those around us. We are neighbors as well as partners.

"Jonathan, a reasonable person could look at what you've done and say you're just a rich kid who has wastefully spent a bunch of your father's money helping a few kids. They could sum you up in this way, and they wouldn't be wrong. On the other hand, you are just a child. You have so much more to do.

"That is why I chose this building. I chose it because, as important as the immaterial is, all of it is built on a physical framework. The physical world is the scaffolding upon which our relationships are grown. Your foundation is funded by profits from this work. The devices you distribute are the creations of engineers and manufacturers. We eat and drink and live and relate only because of the physical production of farmers and roadworkers and crane operators and machinists and truck drivers. Jonathan, the cityscape you see behind me represents the scaffolding of our relationships. It represents the framework upon which the immaterial is established. Shoshana taught me this. I used to think she was pulling me from my work. But my work wasn't made less important by her, it was made more important. You, Jonathan, can never forget it. You need to build our reality, not just embrace those around you. One leads to the other and the other leads to the one.

"Jonathan, you are not physically strong, but your willpower and your focus are amazing. You are going to have rough patches, of every sort. I don't expect you to be perfect or immune to human weakness. I don't *want* you to be perfect. Imperfections often unlock our greatness. It will sound contradictory, but I don't want you to achieve perfection in every little thing. I want you to achieve perfection in everything. If you pull away from the small and every day, you can begin to understand the whole.

"Jonathan, you are 13 years old. Most Bar Mitzvah speeches are a cross between a eulogy and a presidential nomination. You are an impressive child, and so I've delivered something that could pass as either. But you are only 13. I haven't gone through all of this to honor you. I have done it so that you can connect with *this* community. With *my* community. With *Shoshana's* community.

"When you feel weak, these people – this community – can serve as your hands and your ears and heart. They can make you whole.

"Ten years ago, I thought that I'd always regret our failure to preserve Shoshana's ability to have children. I always thought I'd regret not having a child when I could have. But it was Shoshana who taught me the importance of the relationships. It was Shoshana who taught me the importance of self-control. It was Shoshana who helped me understand the path to true success.

"I'm telling you this because I now know, as I stand here today, that you *are* Shoshana's child. Not physically. Not genetically. But in every way that matters. You have inherited the most important parts of her. You are Shoshana's child. We, this community, are *all* Shoshana's children. It is now that I finally realize that I have no regrets.

"Shoshana never knew you, but she would be so proud of who you have become.

"I know I am."

With this, Moses Hassan steps down from his little dais.

The sky is dark now, but the city is ablaze with light. For a long minute, the guests just sit in silence. They just sit, their eyes drifting towards Jonathan Hassan. For his part, Jonathan just sits, physically confined to his chair. He just looks at where his father had stood just moments before.

And then the guests began to rise; one by one. They rise and they make their way towards Jonathan Hassan. They know it is time to introduce themselves to Jonathan, the son of Moses and Shoshana Hassan.

It is time to unlock their own potential.

This week's story isn't about the Torah reading of DEVARIM (Deuteronomy), but about the first two-thirds of the book of DEVARIM.

The book of DEVARIM opens with Moshe making a speech in front of a whole list of places. It seems odd, like he has a huge microphone. However, if we translate the names literally another reality emerges. The words describe the people. The descriptions apply to everybody. Only the last descriptor makes a distinction between people. It separates those who are distinguished and those who lack effort. Through effort, we can be distinguished, even if it is not measurable in human terms.

This introduction is followed by Moshe describing a history of the people. But it is a selective history and one that changes many of the details we encountered before. The history is there to tell a moral story. The story is of the people's growing responsibility.

The first deviation focuses on the communal self-control created by having judges. This parallels Jonathan's use of the PEP machine. It continues with the spies, who parallel Jonathan's blaming others for his own limits. Then G-d commands the people to stop circling Seir and instead go through it. Seir represents the physical and this is paralleled by Moses Hassan's drive to have his son engage in the world.

With the wars against Og and Sihon we see two kings who headed nations that suffered when Amalek did, at the hands of Kedarlaomer. They, like Amalek, bore the same continual grudge from the time of Avraham and the birth of our people. They would weigh on the people so long as they bordered them. The destruction of Og and Sihon parallel's Jonathan's visit to his parents. It is the step they take to overcome their demons. The people are learning the power of their will – which is ultimately represented by G-d's altered plans concerning the two and a half tribes. With will, we can change reality. And Jonathan is learning this power.

The book of *DEVARIM* doesn't stop there. The next Torah reading speaks of G-d's love for the forefathers and their love of him. It parallels Moshe's love of Shoshana. It describes *why* we exist as a people and relate to G-d. But it also shows that our influence is not limited by our lives, but can extend far beyond them. Of course, the power to extend that influence is not our own. It comes from G-d alone. Only He can offer a thousand generations of kindness. There is another trend emerging, though. Rather than a group of individuals, the people are becoming a cohesive whole. In this vein, the Ten Commandments are recast as national commandments, rather than individual ones. This is represented by Jonathan's growing cohesiveness and self-awareness.

In the reading of *EIKEV*, Moshe visits the people's history a third time. This time, it emphasizes that the relationship with G-d is what truly enables us. It teaches us to use the concrete to embrace the timeless. The immaterial, the relationship with G-d, is what actually lasts. We are to circumcise our hearts, so we can serve G-d and realize our full potential. Jonathan learns this lesson through the establishment of his foundation.

In *RE'EH*, we learn to immunize ourselves against relationships that can damage us. We push back against influences that can undermine us – just as Jonathan learns to do. This is followed by *SHOFTIM*, where we are given mechanisms of self-control. Between the choosing of kings and the place of Kohanim and prophets, we learn to regulate our national self.

Jonathan, with his nightly checklist, does the same.

In *KI-TEITZEH*, we learn to hold ourselves together. The laws are laws of neighborliness (among the people and between the people and G-d) and they are critical to making our national selves real. They form a sort of cellular cohesion. Jonathan can only become who he is to be by establishing himself within his community.

In *KI-TAVO*, we come to life. We are given a heart to know, and ears to hear and eyes to see. Like Pinocchio, we become a living nation. We grow into our majority, just as Jonathan becomes a man. He acquires, through his community, his heart, his eyes and his ears. In this reading, we plaster the Torah over rocks – the rocks are the imperfect people, but the national plaster of Torah enables a sort of perfection, even with imperfect building blocks. This recalls the podium.

What follows are covenants, covenants to enable and strengthen the people. These are the covenants that Moshe knows will strengthen his people and enable a better reality. It is, of course, the conclusion of this story.

Moshe's speech is aspirational. We are weak and small, like Jonathan. But we had not, and have not, learned the lessons the boy in this story learned. Jonathan, the child who conquers his demons, acts with will and protects himself. Jonathan who values the immaterial and is enabled by those around him. This Jonathan is the person Moshe hopes we, as a nation, *will* be. But it is not who we are.

We have achieved tremendous things. But we have not realized the fullness of our potential. We have not yet reached the reality that Moshe's last speech holds up as our ideal.

Perhaps, when we do, our small and weak nation will enable the nations of the world.

Perhaps, when we do, we will witness the coming of Moshiach.

Va'etchanan: The Life of Charlie Barnes

The morning that changed my life started like all the others. I left the small apartment I shared with six other immigrants and made my way to work. The elevator down to the bottom floor of the building creaked as it always did. As the door to the building opened, I was greeted by the smell of rain. This wasn't the refreshing of rain you might find in other places. Instead, the rain just brought out the worst in the city. The smell of rotting vegetables, of rotting streets and of rotting buildings was empowered by the wet that washed over the place on a regular basis. As I had many times before, I asked myself why I was still here.

I knew the answer, but I asked nonetheless.

I made my way through the empty market. The smells of the city were stronger here. Trash left over from the night before festered in the moist morning air. I kept walking, past boarded-up buildings, pound shops, and charity stores selling a variety of worthless knickknacks.

Finally, I came to my destination. It stood out from its surroundings, at least externally. It was an old manor house, with elegant lines and beautifully fashioned features. It had been built during a better age, when the city had been a center for wool production. A wealthy family had lived there. They had long since left. Now, the house was an old-age home for those who had no other options.

As I drew close to the door, a familiar smell greeted me. Not just the vague urine-smell of every old age home. No, this was something worse. I knew the cause. The patients weren't properly cleaned, laundry wasn't done, floors and bathrooms weren't sanitized. The home was a disgusting place. Once grand rooms had been subdivided by cheap walls and fine wooden floors had been covered by cheap and poorly applied linoleum. Old fluorescent bulbs provided what passed for illumination, which was probably better than revealing the filth that had consumed the place. Only the desperate would find their way here. Only the hated would be assigned such a home.

Any decent family would find something better for their elders.

I'd started working here seven years earlier. I'd left my home is Poland. I'd left behind my wife and my baby. I'd come to England to work. I barely spoke any English, then. But I'd gone to the Job Centre and they'd placed me here, as a cleaner. Those first months I thought of it as a place of transition. I'd work here, in this place, until I could leave. Then I'd move up, my improving English granting me a path towards something better. I'd earn more money, then. I'd send more home. Eventually, my family would come to me. Maybe we'd buy a little flat and live happily ever after.

It hadn't worked out that way.

The patients suffered dementia of all sorts. The home 'specialized' in their care. Many of the patients weren't just sweet old people with scrambled minds. Quite a few of them were aggressive, mean, paranoid and vindictive. It wasn't random. They had been assigned to this place because nobody cared to find them something better. Sometimes this was their own fault. The staff hated them, often with good reason. Most didn't actively hurt patients, but they actively neglected them. A few went further than that – allowing their anger and frustration to show in physical abuse. The staff were there for only one reason: to collect their pay and then move on to something better. Most came and went in only a few months. The management didn't seem to mind. They kept their eyes shut, they kept costs low, and they kept the profits coming in.

That's why I stayed. I didn't like the patients. I didn't like the staff. But the patients needed *somebody* who would do *something* for them. My wife hated what I was doing. I wasn't moving up the pay scale. I wasn't getting a flat. I wasn't bringing her to England. I wasn't helping her raise my son.

I was doing something for people nobody else wanted to help, though. And although I couldn't possibly keep up with the demands of the 200+ people who lived in the manor, I did my best. I worked hard, swimming against the stream of disgust produced by the elderly patients. I did it because somebody had to at least try.

I paid, every day, for my decision.

Every day had been the same. For seven years, there had been the same smells. The same dimly lit corridors. The same iffy maintenance. The same angry patients – some of whom would scream epithets at me – the Pollak who had come to take their jobs. The staff had changed, but none of them would speak to me. I was beneath them. I meant nothing. And yet somehow, I couldn't allow myself to escape.

Then, everything changed.

I was cleaning a hallway. I was surrounded by the strong smell of bleach and I was swishing my mop back and forth, pushing against the odors that defined the place. Then I looked up and I saw a patient. But unlike all the others, his face was glowing with some internal light.

He wasn't looking at me. He was looking *beyond* me.

His eyes were filled with joy.

I watched him as he approached. And I watched him as he passed, silently, down the hall. He was following some vision of paradise. I kept moping that day, like any other. But the vision of him filled my mind. In seven years of labor, I had never seen anybody like him.

The next day, scrubbing away at stains in another hall, I saw him again. He had that same beatific face. That same joy. Only this time he was speaking. He had stopped, right next to me, and he was talking into the air. He was describing a scene. Something involving a woman named Rebecca. I stopped to listen. The story was cogent and clear. It seemed Rebecca was a scientist of some sort. She had adapted farming practices somewhere, yielding regular and sustainable crops where none had been possible before. The way the man spoke, it seemed like she was changing lives. It seemed like she was working miracles for people who had been kept low for hundreds of years. I didn't have any idea what it meant. When he finished, he shuffled off, just as he had the day before.

The next day, I saw him again. He stopped again. He narrated a story about a man named Jason. The day after that, the story was about a man named Hugh.

They were stories of hope and of impact and of change.

I figured the stories must reflect some kind of Alzheimer's. I figured he must be living in the past. I asked the secretary for the man's name and learned it was Charlie Barnes. On my way home that third night, I stopped by the library. I looked him up and found him. He had been born 78 years earlier. He had worked in a wool mill until it closed in the 1990s. The local newspaper had chosen to interview him when he'd been laid off. He had had no siblings, wife or children.

His parents had died years earlier. No Hughs or Rebeccas or Jasons were mentioned in the piece. He was an unconnected man, cut adrift by the loss of his mill job. There was no mention of sparkling eyes.

I went back to work the next day. Charlie shared another story. He was still talking to no-one and looking at nothing. But he was describing something beautiful. I stopped and listened. When he was done, we both moved on. He continued to shuffle through the halls and I carried on with my cleaning.

For the first time, I started to look forward to my work. I thought others might feel the same. I asked others on the staff what they thought of him. Nobody else seemed to notice him, though. Plus, they didn't want to talk to me. He brought light to the entire place, but nobody else saw it. To them, he was just another worthless patient.

His was a light only *I* could see.

One day, when I was replacing a broken fluorescent tube, he came towards me. I glanced down at him, waiting for him to stop and narrate a story. He did stop. But he didn't share a story; his eyes weren't looking into the distance. Instead, he focused on me. His eyes focused on me. They were ablaze with joy and appreciation. And then he said one word, "Jaroslaw."

It was my name. He said my name.

With that, he turned and shuffled down the hall, like he had every other day.

I knew then that he saw something in me. Even my wife had never looked at me in that way. I went home, navigating through the market and heading towards my flat where I still lived with six other immigrants. But now I saw the market differently. I didn't notice the grime and the smells and the rot. Instead, I saw the few hopeful kids and the stall operators trying desperately to share the flavors of their homelands. I saw their hopes, and not their horrors.

For the first time in my life, I knew I was important. All because a demented old man had looked at me and said my name.

I came back the next day, hoping to hear another story. I cleaned the halls, but I did not see the man. For the first time in weeks, I did not see the man. The entire day I worked, eagerly waiting for an encounter with the man with the face of light. But he was not there.

When I asked the secretary about him, she told me, in a flat and uncaring voice, "Charlie Barnes is dead." The state was paying for his funeral.

Charlie Barnes would be buried the next day.

I went home that night. The city weighed on me again. I had had a moment of joy and of hope. But now it was gone. I felt the weight of my reality more heavily than ever before. For the first time in years, I considered leaving my job. After all, I did not owe these old people my life. Hadn't they earned their sentence? Was it my fault they had no families who cared? Did my wife have to stay, far from me, because of them?

I came to my flat. The seven tenants shared one bathroom and one kitchen. We never spoke. They passed through, spending a few months there and then moving on to something better. But I never left. I stayed there, punishing myself to help people who would never even thank me.

Now Charlie was gone, and there was no reason to keep sacrificing.

It wasn't that simple, though, I had a sense of obligation. Charlie had seen something. He had brought light to my life, so I owed *him* something in return. I spent some of my meager savings and I rented a local church. It was a huge space, long since abandoned with the changing mores of the city. I would hold a memorial service there. A celebration of a man nobody else seemed to know.

I placed an obituary in the local paper. I used his name. I provided a brief outline of his career. I mentioned, ever so briefly, that he spread stories of hope. And I mentioned, in the last line, that there would be memorial service for the man with the shining face.

The next day, and the day after that, I continued working at the home – just as before. I trudged through the filth and I imagined Charlie Barnes coming down the hall, bringing joy to my darkness.

Now, seven days have passed. It is time for the memorial service.

I walk up the rundown street, heading towards the worn-looking church at what had once been a prominent corner. The lights are on in the building, shining through the dust-covered stained-glass windows. It is a beautiful building, but its purpose has been lost. It has always stood empty. Every time I passed it, it had been empty. I push open the heavy door, expecting an empty room. But the room is full. There are hundreds of people there. I looked behind me and I see more are coming. They are abuzz with conversation. The room is aglow with energy.

Hundreds of people have come to the wake of a man who had no family.

I begin to walk through the sanctuary. I introduce myself and others introduce themselves to me. I meet a Jason and I meet a Hugh. For every story I have heard, I meet a person who matches the tale.

I ask them why they are there. They all have the same answer: Charlie Barnes had seen them. With his eyes of light, he had seen them and they had known they had a future and a purpose. They had known they weren't worthless and meaningless. Charlie Barnes' belief had changed their lives.

They tell me they had been drawn to the paper that day. They had seen the obituary. They had known that they had to come.

I ask them for their stories, then. And they tell me about their lives. Their eyes all sparkle with the light of potential. But none have lived the stories Charlie had told to me. I couldn't understand what he had shared with me. Where did his stories come from? What were they about?

As I circulate through the room, I meet only one Rebecca. She is a child, no older than 6. I ask if she had met Charlie and she says 'no.'

But her parents had. Charlie had brought them together.

I smile, confused.

Then, out of the blue, the little girl tells me that she loves plants. It is then that I understand.

Charlie hadn't been sharing stories of the past. He had been sharing stories of the future. In his old age, in his dementia, he was seeing the impact his life would have.

He had been blessed with a sort of prophecy.

I know, now, that I have inherited his vision. I know what awaits Rebecca and Hugh and Jason and all the others. I feel the spark of Charlie's eyes entering my own. I know these people's stories. And I know that I, like Charlie, will be able to see others and recognize the potential in their lives.

Men and women and children step up then, to the podium. They speak about their time with Charlie. They speak of the time when he saw them and changed their lives. One by one they rise up and share what they experienced. Eventually there are no speakers left. None but me.

The crowd looks to me, expectant and waiting. They know I placed the obituary.

I cannot share their futures with them. Instead, when I rise to the podium, I speak not of my individual experience, but of *our* experience. I speak of the possibilities that may be unleashed by all of us *together*. I speak of what Charlie saw in *us*, not just each one of us.

Just like that I establish a community. Charlie's community.

A man comes up to me then. He introduces himself. He is a solicitor, the man responsible for Charlie's estate. Charlie, who had had no family, had left behind a substantial amount of money.

Charlie had named *me* as his inheritor.

I am confused. When could he have named me? Can a demented old man write out a will?

Without prompting, the lawyer shows me the document. My full name is there, written in clear script. At the bottom, there is a date. The will had been signed seven years earlier. It had been signed the same day I had come to England.

I wish, suddenly, that Charlie had told me my story. I wish suddenly, that he had defined my path. But even as the thought crosses my mind, I know what I must do.

I will buy the old age home. I will replace the staff. I will refurbish the building. I will bring my family over. I will care for those who have no one to care for them.

But I will do more than that. I will follow in the footsteps of Charlie Barnes, finding hope where others see nothing of value.

With these people, with his people, this rotting city will be transformed.

Together, we will cultivate the seeds of life.

At the beginning of the Torah reading of *VE'ETCHANAN*, Moshe remembers that he had critiqued G-d's choice to exclude him from the land. G-d had responded by offering Moshe the chance to go up to the peak of Pisgah and look down from that place. While he is there, G-d tells him to look in all four directions, not just towards the land.

The question is, why?

Pisgah first comes up in the song *AZ YASHIR YISRAEL. AZ YASHIR MOSHE*, sung upon the people's crossing of the sea, shows the people walking on dry land through a break in the sea. But *AZ YASHIR YISRAEL* describes the people as the water. They flow through the desert and references are given to the giving of the Torah, the death of the spies and the worship of *BAAL PEOR*. At the end of the song, the waters flow up to and over *ROSH HAPISGAH* (the top of Pisgah). This seems impossible, water does not flow upwards. But, of course, these waters are not literal, but spiritual.

When Moshe climbs this hill and looks in all four directions, he is seeing the impact of his own life. He is seeing the future of the people he has rescued. He is seeing where they will flow, having climbed the great heights. Moshe will not cross the Jordan, but he does see what comes after he has left our physical reality.

Moshe does not simply rest then, his vision in hand. He still continues to act and to shape the people. In a way, he fights against the limits of his vision – or any vision whatsoever. In the following chapter (chapter 4), we are reminded no fewer than five times of the limits of images. The act of creating images leads to the worship of the sun and the moon and then, eventually, to the worship of the work of man. The process is one in which imagination in consumed. Images form and limit our imagination. When we create them, when we see them, we can't appreciate the formless reality of G-d or the formless potential of our own people.

Despite Moshe's vision – despite him *seeing* our future – we are to be a people open to imagination. It is a statement of Moshe's greatness that he can see the future and push back against the limits that vision might impose.

Moshe breaks his speech here, just once, to act. He designates the cities of refuge. He doesn't establish them (*KARITEM*). He only designates (*YAVDEEL*) them. Moshe is a protector, a shepherd. The cities of refuge are what he chooses as his personal legacy.

What comes next is the Ten Declarations. But they have been changed. Gone is the panic of the first version (Shemot/Ex 20:1-13). It has been replaced with deliberation (Dev/Deut 5:6-17). This parallels the American experience with the Constitution. In our modern understanding, it was produced with deliberation. At the time, the process was far more chaotic and far from certain. This change speaks to a shift in the commandments themselves. This second set of commandments no longer speak to individuals, they speak to the nation as a whole. Alternations are made, alterations which reflect this change. We are all a part of the Ten Declarations just as Americans are all a part of the Constitution. We are signatories to a document signed long before we were born. We are parties to a covenant established thousands of years ago. This reality can only be true when we come together as a people.

Moshe is not just pushing against a vision; he is trying to fashion the people as *a people*.

Then we are reminded once again to listen. Only if we listen, and pass on the words which we have heard, can we realize the blessings that await us. It is this chain of memory, not of artifacts, that links our people together.

The reading ends with an explanation of sorts. Moshe says G-d will reward those who love him and keep his commandments. The rewards will last for a thousand generations. And he says that those who hate him, will be repaid face to face. In a way, it is an answer to the question at the beginning of the reading.

Moshe is being prevented from entering the land. G-d is repaying his act of rebellion – face-to-face. But a thousand generations of kindness still remain as Moshe's reward. A thousand generations of hope, visible from the peaks of Pisgah, remain as his reward.

The story of Charlie Barnes parallels this reading. Just as Moshe looks down from *PISGAH*, Charlie sees the impact of his life. He continues, even then, to push against reality. He continues to try to better what has already been established. Just as Moshe designates cities, Charlie chooses a man who can pass on his belief in others. And just as Moshe wills a collective reality into reality, Charlie's memorial service serves as the formation of a new community – a community that will transform a world of rot. It is not a community built on artifact. It is a community built on memory and on words.

We all falter. We all die.

It should be our hope to realize the sort of life Moshe realized. It should be our hope to be repaid for our hatred, face-to-face. This should be our hope – so that we may be rewarded for our love with a thousand generations of kindness.

May our legacies be strengthened by those we have blessed.

h/t Eli for his insights into nursing home workers and for modeling the character of Jaroslaw.

Eikev: The General

The bunker is forty feet long, ten feet wide, and strongly reinforced. It is a small, but important space. It is buried far beneath the earth, and it is dominated by a single long table. Above the table, a single fluorescent bulb burns. And at the head of the table stands a dark-skinned man. His face somehow seems pale in the thinly lit space.

The man, the table and the bunker have been in place for decades, living testaments to a war that has not yet ended. The General is an old man now, well into his eighties. But he is still strong. He stands strong, his back straight, his eyes full of power and purpose and dedication.

As he watches, waiting, standing, his people begin to enter the room.

One by one, they make their way in and seat themselves, silently, along the sides of the long table. The General watches them enter. He watches their faces. He knows, even though he stands erect, that they cannot stand erect. They are burdened. They are frightened. They are exhausted. And they are desperate.

Years of conflict have taken their toll.

Before long, the thin drizzle of people comes to a stop. The table, which had been brimming with personnel in decades past, is only half full. One by one, the General's eyes linger over the empty seats. He remembers those who sat in those places. He remembers their decades of companionship and dedication. Today, another seat is empty. The occupant – a once notable commander – did not die in battle. He was simply overcome by the inevitability of age.

The General's eyes come to rest on the man's seat. He feels the urge to mourn. He feels the desperation of his people gnawing at his soul. How long must they fight?

The General feels their desperation calling to him. It invites him, after years of resistance, to bend, to sit and to surrender. But he cannot.

Their freedom is still not complete.

At that moment, the General sets aside his agenda and his plans. He must push, instead, against the desperation.

He begins to speak.

"My dear compatriots, I feel the need to remember why we are here."

Tired faces watch him. He takes a deep breath and then shares, yet again, the story that has propelled his little nation for so long.

"As you know, I grew up a slave. I was born in a cashew orchard and my mother, her labor complete, simply bound me to her front and continued with her work. She was allowed no rest, even upon the birth of a child. When I was only two-years old, I joined the ranks of her people. My job was simple. I was to carry small bags of cashew fruits – picked by my elders – to giant collection bins. Most two-year-olds, in most places, might not have been able to manage such a job. But we were slaves, all of us. The pain of resistance was something we could all feel. That pain enabled even toddlers to learn simple jobs and to carry them out for hours on end. We knew there was no choice. We had only pain or work. My only joy came from my mother. She would sing to me in the night. She would do her best to hide my shortcomings from the masters. And, when she could do nothing more, she would smile to me from across the orchard. When she was otherwise powerless, she would let me know that I was loved.

"We were slaves. Everything our people produced was given to our masters. Of course, we were not only robbed of the wealth of our land, we were robbed of our identity. We belonged to no nation, no people, no tribe. We were just the slaves, imported from faraway lands, and set to work. We did not share even a language.

"When I was ten years old, a man led a rebellion against his masters. He had been an administrator for the overlords. He had kept the books for the masters; managing the movement of slaves, material, machinery and goods from place to place within their domain. Others had rebelled before him, but he was the first to have the tools necessary for such a rebellion to succeed. That man mustered the slaves on his plantation. He mustered them and he slaughtered the overseers in that place. He kept going then, extending his influence and pushing back against our oppression.

"We fought for four long years then. The men fought, shielding the women and the children and the elderly from the overseers. The men fought. And then they established a new city on a small island off the coast. It was a place for the children, it was a place for the women. It was a place for the elderly. It was a place of safety. It was where our past and our future lay, separate from the fields of battle. We called it Harmony.

"We drove the enemy from our lands. But they were not so easily defeated. After all, we were valuable to them. They intended to keep us as their chattel. They gathered a fleet of dozens of ships and hundreds of thousands of men. They set sail for our land.

"I was drafted then. I was fourteen, but every man, woman and child who could fight was wanted. Only our weakest people were left in Harmony. My mother, once again with child, was in that city. My mother who had carried me in the field and protected me from the oppression of our masters. My mother who had loved me when she had nothing else to give. She was in that city. But we were not. We wanted to meet our enemies on the field of battle. We trusted they would have the honor to fight us there.

They had no honor.

"The enemy's ships came. But they did not attack our armies. Instead, they lay siege to that city. They were clever. Their armies were safe, on their ships in the sea. We had no ships. They wanted our army to come, to try do battle against them there. To try to cross the shallows in a useless assault. They wanted us to be cut down by their guns until we ceased our rebellion. We were not that stupid. We knew they were offering us a trap; a trap we could not afford to spring. Even I, a 14-year-old boy, understood that fighting for Harmony meant death for our people. So, we watched. We all just watched as Harmony began to starve. But we did not attack. Our enemy grew impatient. They began to fire on the city. Still, we watched. I knew my mother was there. I knew so many of the mothers were there. I knew they were dying of starvation and fire. But we watched. Our greater purpose demanded it.

"We watched as the enemy destroyed the young, the old and the weak. We watched, suffering in our souls. In that unfought battle, our people were born. We were born of our anger and our defeat and our shared loss. Harmony was destroyed. But then, their hostages gone, the enemy had no choice by to attack us directly. That was when they came ashore with their armies.

"Our people, vastly outnumbered and facing an enemy with machine guns and artillery, finally met them on the field of battle. We had rifles and knives. We had rifles and knives and anger and will and commitment. It was then that the leader of the slaves, the administrator with the records, told me that I was his son. He knew what would happen next. It was during that battle that we were truly forged as a nation. We joined together, our individual wills growing in their unity. We defeated the enemy. We stole their guns and turned them against them. We broke their will and their pride. We came to life. We came to life as a people. We had finally thrown off our oppressors."

The General looks around the room. The faces there are younger than his. All of them are younger. Only one person, his own wife, had been there on that critical day. He looks around, then continues to speak.

"My father died in that battle. At 14, as an orphan, I became the leader of our people. But our war did not stop then. The threat of our enemy has remained on the edges of our reality. They have not invaded our land, but still they threaten our will and our freedom.

"That is why we have learned to trust only in ourselves. There are those who call themselves allies. They offer us food and wealth and support. They want us to believe that a relationship with them is somehow more real than the guns and the bullets that our hands can touch. But we know better. They too want to rob us of our will, and of our identity. They want us to conform to their rules and their values. They want us to put aside our anger and our pride. But we know that they want us to put aside the very things that give us our identity.

"This, my compatriots, is why we stand alone. This is why we keep fighting. We must depend only on ourselves. Because to do otherwise would be to surrender. It would be to trade our identity and our will for the cheap promise of wealth. We were forged in battle. We came to life in battle. We can never surrender the determination that

44

gave us life. No matter our hardship, any who threaten our independence will never be satisfied by our surrender.

"And we will, soon, be free."

The General looks around the room. He is proud, he is strong. Sixty-five years of war and he is still strong. He looks around the room and sees the hungry and thin faces of his compatriots. But he also sees their hope. He sees their pride. He knows that they would suffer, but they will remain – free and proud – despite their hardships.

The meeting continues then. The planning and the strategy. The agenda as it had existed before. Everything is dedicated to the war. Everything is dedicated to keeping the enemy at bay. Such dedication takes tremendous planning and oversight.

The General considers: once, their wealth had gone to their oppressors. In a way, it still does.

All they have gained is their identity and their will.

When the meeting is complete, the General retires from the bunker. He has his quarters underground, adjacent to the meeting space. He comes to his room, a small space appropriate for a wartime commander. In this place, this private place, he allows himself to be old and tired.

He is old and tired, but his pride remains strong.

His wife follows after him. Once their door closes, she puts her hand on his shoulder and turns him towards her.

"My husband," she says, solemnly, "Your story was not complete."

He cocks his head at her, confused.

"After the massacre at Harmony, an army was mustered. It was an army raised from a nearby nation, in reaction to the crimes against us. While we fought our masters, they attacked the fleets of our oppressors. That day, they came ashore, surrounding our enemies. We fought, bravely. But it was *they* who won the war."

The General grimaces slightly. It is not the story his people need.

But then she continues, "Then they offered us help. They offered us support. We needed only to conform to their treaties and their moral codes. We needed only to recognize their assistance and give thanks for it. They offered us blessing. But we did not accept their offer. So, they embargoed us. They accused us of war crimes against our enemies and against our own people. They afflicted us, hoping we will join them in their moral reality. They offered to empower us with their laws and their technologies and their investments. But we refuse them. My husband, generations of our people could have been living lives of fulfillment. They still can. All we must do is step away from our anger. All we must do is give up on the emptiness of your freedom."

The General smiles then. For he knows that he will never trade his will and his pride and his independence for the false and empty promise of wealth.

"All we need to do," his wife insists, "Is reach towards them and allow them to embrace us."

But the General does not listen. He just turns away.

And his wife silently waits for his time – the time of resistance – to pass.

In the Torah reading of *EIKEV*, Moshe retells the Sin of the Calf. The Sin of the Calf was a sin of collective self-worship. At its core, the golden idol was formed of the earrings of the community. It represents the power formed by the community members hearing each other. It represents the community, but it excludes G-d. We know this because the people worship the calf by playing.

When you play in worship, you are worshiping yourself.

With the Sin of the Calf, the people imagined, just as the General in the story does, that they are responsible for their own freedom.

They erase the role of their greatest ally: G-d Himself.

The Sin of the Calf is not the end of the story, though. In this Torah reading, the Sin of the Calf is wrapped in a challenge: the challenge of recognizing G-d's role. Here, the 40 years in the desert aren't just a punishment for the sin of the spies, they are a part of this challenge. As the Torah says: "He afflicted you... so you might know that man does not live by bread alone, but from everything that comes from the mouth of the Lord." (Dev 8:3).

In the story of the General, as in Moshe's speech, the people are burdened for decades because they will not admit the importance of their allies.

But there is a path to blessing. We are commanded to circumcise our hearts (Dev 10:16). To understand this, we need to understand the function of blood in the Torah. Blood enables our bodies; it is defined as the physical soul of meat. It gives us our potential, unifying our cells in life. Our hearts, in turn, power that potential. With circumcision, we open our hearts to Divine guidance. We remove our resistance to G-d's commandments. We allow G-d's will to be expressed through us. We give up something of our freedom, just as the General's allies insist that he does.

We must do what the General cannot. We, like his wife, must come to understand that the result will not be a lack of individuality or freedom. G-d is not seeking to rob us. Instead, the result will be an opportunity for true fulfillment.

Moshe, like the General's wife, understands what must happen to bring us to that reality. We only need to turn towards our ally to initiate the relationship we so badly need. We see this in the aftermath of the Sin of the Calf. In this telling, Moshe replaces the Divine Ten Commandments, written by the finger of G-d, with very human Ten Commandments crafted by him. These commandments are housed in a wooden box. The gold of the *ARON KODESH* (Holy Ark) is not mentioned. Instead, Shittim trees, literally 'grudge trees', are used to contain the core of our Divine relationship.

Moshe recasts our human limitations and uses them to form a relationship with G-d. He gets past our human anger to form something more valuable and rewarding. He gives us the beginnings of a path towards our ultimate redemption.

The reading ends as it begins, with the promise of blessings. But these blessings contain a warning. The land we are entering is not like Egypt, which is irrigated by the foot. The foot represents a man's will. Our new land, our new reality, is not one in which our needs are fulfilled through our efforts. No, this land is a land which drinks the waters of heaven (Dev 11:10-11). Something more than dedication is required.

It is not enough for us to struggle, just as it is not enough for the General's people to struggle. We can only find our redemption in our greatest ally.

It is only by following G-d's commandments and loving Him with all of our heart and all of our soul that we can be blessed. (Dev 11:13)

Shabbat Shalom.

The story above borrows from a group of historical models. It most closely models the Haitian slave revolt: the first successful, human-driven, slave rebellion. It was, for a critical period, led by a slave who had been an administrator. The Haitian rebellion was driven by anger. Every European on the island was killed and for forty years after the French were driven from the island, the Haitian government dedicated all of its resources to war. But that is not the only model. The story also borrows from North Korea (with its policy of complete self-sufficiency) and. And it borrows from Eritrea, a country which broke off from Ethiopia and was locked in a war of total resistance for years afterwards.

It is my hope that such troubled nations find their allies and find their blessings – emerging from their darkness and overcoming the angers that forged them.

Re'eh: The Kansas City Apocalypse

By the time I was 40, I'd been through pretty much every sort of therapy available on planet Earth. There had been the obvious ones, like cognitive therapy, behavioral therapy and psychoanalysis. But my attempts at self-repair went deeper. I'd also done acceptance therapy, art therapy, group psychotherapy and even eye movement desensitization and reprocessing therapy. Don't ask me about that one. When it came to therapy, I'd seen it all.

But none of it had fixed me.

In my desperation, I'd gone beyond the psychological world. I'd become a drug user, switching from Oxy to heroin and even, when I really wanted to mess with my world view, to acid.

But none of it worked.

I was a broken man. I was unfixable.

I knew why I was unfixable. My parents had been psychotic religious fundamentalists who read the Bible literally. And not just the Christian Bible, but the Hebrew one. They rejected evolution. They rejected science. They resisted the modern world. They dreamed of casting stones upon sinners. They spoke about when they would destroy the rebellious city, or what they'd do to the false prophet. Heck, they even named me Enoch, after the man who walked with G-d and never died.

When I was very young, I was a part of it. I was a part of it all. But I didn't live up to my name. I began to see cracks early on. They kept me separated from the wider world, cut me off from it. But I learned nonetheless. I'd always had a bit of a rebellious streak and I knew exactly the kinds of things they didn't accept. I actually read Charles Darwin; his book secretly hidden in my pillow. I hid lots of books there, wrapped in the warm smell of cotton. I learned about democracy and the freedom of speech and the benefits of a society with the free exchange of ideas – a melting pot of thought that bubbled up and rewarded the best mankind had to offer.

My parents eventually found the Darwin. They found all the books. And they didn't spare the rod. Their love of me was *contingent* on my embrace of their world. And so, gradually, they began to push me away. But then I grew up a bit more, and became the one thing they couldn't accept. That was the first therapy I underwent. They arranged it. I went voluntarily. I wanted to fix myself. But I couldn't.

So, they rejected me, totally.

I was an abomination to them.

The real problem was that I was an abomination to myself. I know it makes no sense. I didn't agree with their ideas. I argued with them. I pushed back against them. But my arguments were *intellectual*. In my *soul*, I knew my parents were right. I knew I *shouldn't* have a place in the world. That's where the drug use started.

I guess, in that way, the beatings had done their job. My parents had gotten into me so effectively that I couldn't begin to love myself. Like many junkies, I became a great philosopher. Sometimes I wonder if perhaps the philosophy is the cause of our addictions, instead of the other way around. Perhaps we're all broken by the distance between what we believe and what we feel.

No matter the cause, I was a broken man and there was nothing I could do to fix myself.

Then, the world ended.

It had been one Wednesday evening in the middle of winter. I'd been taking a break from rehab and was going through a brief period of 'alternative living arrangements'. In other words, I was high and homeless. But I lived in Kansas City. If you don't know Kansas City, it gets cold in winter. Deadly cold. Actually, living on the streets would be a death sentence. I wasn't suicidal, yet. Kansas City has an underground city-like area called SubTropolis. It has roads and warehouses and even little factories. There, the temperatures stay within a very comfortable range all year round. Get in there and you can stay safe, like a bear in hibernation. Even high, I was smart enough to know I needed to be in the SubTropolis, not outside.

Of course, getting in isn't easy. The place is a bit like Fort Knox, with huge doors buried in the sides of the hill it is under. There are very limited opportunities for homeless ingress. I had a friend, though, from my Drug Addicts Anonymous group. He loaned me a pass. That's why, every night, I'd drive my old beater of a car through the opening on the side of the hill, park it in some empty corner and go to sleep. Every night, I was miserable. Almost every night, I was high. But I was never cold.

Then, one Wednesday night, I woke up feeling like there wasn't enough air. It wasn't that *all* the air was gone, it was that a whole lot of it seemed to be. I sat up and rolled down my car window, expecting more air to rush into the car. Instead, more air seemed to rush *out* of the car. I had no idea what was going on and so I turned on the car and drove to the entrance of SubTropolis. The car was certainly running rough, like it didn't have enough air either. Nonetheless, I waved my pass in front of the reader and with a rush of air the huge gate opened.

I expected to see the bright lights of a truck yard surrounded by a dark forest. Instead what I saw was fire. Everything was on fire. I could smell charcoal and sulfur filling the air. I glanced towards the sky and saw fireballs descending from it. They were striking the city, like it was a modern-day Sodom and Gomorrah. They were laying waste to the world around me.

I just sat in my car, stunned. Still stunned, I waved my pass again, closed the gates, and drove back to my parking spot.

I was low on oxygen. I was weak and I was scared. The world was on fire and I needed to survive.

I didn't realize it then, but that was the first time in my adult life that I wasn't miserably depressed.

That night was truly catastrophic. But others had survived, both within SubTropolis and outside of it. People had been working underground, in SubTropolis. Others got lucky, running to the underground city as the sky around them opened up. Still others had been buried deep enough in cellars to survive when the fires rained down.

None of us really knew what had happened. What we did know was that everything we could see had been eliminated. Farms. Stores. Homes. Everything. The sun itself had been erased beyond the darkness of the smoke.

But I had been reborn.

You see, I was unique among the survivors. Most of them had simply been working the overnight shift in the underground warehouses; packing and moving boxes. Others had been driving nearby, for one reason or another. As the fires came, they rushed to SubTropolis. Still others had simply been up late, playing games in cellars when the end of the world came.

They were people, good, bad and indifferent. They weren't special in any way. I was. Between my itinerant jobs and my auto-didactic education, I knew something about pretty much everything.

I knew rudimentary first aid, some basics about water treatment, a bit about construction. And, because of my self-loathing, I was the one who knew better than most how to talk people through pain and fear. I was the one they came to for counseling, and they *all* needed counseling.

Most importantly, I had a vision. I wanted to see the world reborn. It was a world that didn't need me when it had been humming along. But now, it was a world that couldn't survive without me. This was why I couldn't let it die.

It wasn't long before I became the leader of SubTropolis.

The rain of fire passed within a day. The blazes within a few weeks. But the darkness didn't go. We didn't see the sun for months. We sent out search parties. We gathered supplies from the remains of houses. We filtered the dirty waters of the Missouri river, at least as best we could. We suffered terribly. Not just from hunger or injury, but from simple sickness. Heart attacks were left untreated; there was nothing we could do. We had almost no medication and what we did have we could only use in the most rudimentary ways. None of us were doctors.

As the sun began to be revealed – which we didn't know would happen at the time – we began to plan a farm. There were young men and women, who had been working in the warehouses, who had grown up on farms. We didn't have combines or complex statistical analysis of crop placement. But we had some basic know-how and we had some seeds buried among the SubTropolis food storage warehouses.

Next, we realized more than just another generation of plants, we needed another generation of *people*. Very few children had survived. They hadn't been out in the middle of the night. They hadn't been working in cellars or underground caverns. Children had almost been erased from our world. So, they became a part of our vision. As in so many disaster movies, reproduction became core to our understanding of survival.

The idea of children gave us hope. And so, in the face of despair, we kept going. Our little city, populated with stragglers, refused to die.

***

I Chausiku Mwangi, have heard the voice of Moloch. He spoke to me last night from among the clouds of darkness. The clouds of fire that gathered at the height of the noonday sun. Moloch spoke, casting his voice from the heavens. And, once again, he demanded our fealty.

I quavered in fear before him. He has attacked our world. He has cast us under his shadow. And he has done so because we have rebelled against him.

Moloch demands our sacrifice. He demands our humility. He demands our fealty. He demands our trust.

Humanity must come together – all of humanity – and we must dedicate our future to Moloch. We must dedicate it so that Moloch does not take it. We must dedicate it so that the darkness can be lifted, so that the crops can return and so that our lives may be restored.

I Chausiku Mwangi, have heard the voice of Moloch. Men tried to stop his voice. They tried to drug me into unawareness, into a world of silence. They tried to lock out the prophecies of Moloch. But they could not succeed. I spoke of Moloch. I spoke of the destruction. But they did not hear. And so, they were not warned.

But now, now that the destruction I prophesied has come, the voice of Moloch shines through. Now, they remember my warnings. Now, they heed my voice.

It is I, Chausiku Mwangi, who hears the voice of the Dark King. It is I who spreads his words throughout our world. It is I who have given life and voice to the other prophets of this King. Together, we share our vision. Together, we know what Moloch demands.

It is only through sacrifice, only through dedication, that Moloch will relent.

It is only by showing we can give up all that humankind will survive.

We weep, filled with sadness. But there is hope too. There is joy in sacrifice. There is joy in purification.

This is the word of Moloch. May his word be spread.

***

We planted our first crops as the sun began to appear from behind the blanket of smoke. The earth smelled burnt, but it held the promise of future life. We planted our first crops and we celebrated the first of our pregnancies. I was like a tribal leader. There was no voting, no selection. I was simply the one who made the decisions and others respected the decisions I made.

We began to hear from survivors further afield. There were towns here and there. In what used to be Kansas City there were survivors in the sub-basements of the airport and downtown. Because of the size and resources of SubTropolis, we grew to encompass these places. They came under my rule.

But we heard of other settlements, further afield. The old underground Strategic Oil Reserves in Louisiana and Texas were settled. They offered immense and invaluable stockpiles of oil and gas. Others had food. Some had banks of seeds. And yet others offered pockets of skilled people.

We began to reach out to them. One survivor made ham radios. We sent trucks out to the settlements we could find, and we sent his radios with those trucks.

We were forming a community of communities. We were building a new reality. SubTropolis, with its simple scale and variety of goods, had become the nexus of a new world.

It was a new world that was only a seed, though. It was not yet a reality.

***

I am an apostle of Chausiku Mwangi. We have suffered the vengeance of Moloch. We must sacrifice to him. Only then will he relent. I have seen the sacrifice. I have seen the dedications. I, myself, have dedicated my eldest son to the alien god. And I have seen the coming of light. There are those who deny the blessings of Moloch, but we remove them. They cannot be allowed to survive. They anger Moloch.

They anger Moloch even as the sun returns and his anger abates.

The fires have passed. Moloch is blessing our efforts.

This is why I have traveled so far, carrying the prophecies of Chausiku Mwangi to the remnants of mankind. They, the notebooks inscribed in the hand of Chausiku Mwangi himself, are my most precious belongings. They are my gift to mankind. I am carrying them even across the immense seas. Despite the danger, I must carry this prophecy to all corners of the earth.

There are those who challenge us, but they cannot be allowed to survive.

We have dedicated too much to spurn the blessings of the Dark King.

***

The first harvest is almost upon us. The smell of life fills our little crack of land, resisting the death that still surrounds us. It is then that the radios began to fill with a new vision. From far and near, the crackle of strange prophecies came over the airwaves. They claimed that the darkness was brought on by an alien power. They called it a god. They called it Moloch.

And they claimed that Moloch demanded the sacrifice of children.

I could not believe them. How could we build a future without children?

They claimed that we must show our trust and our faith, and that only then would we be blessed.

All I heard was the insanity of my parents.

They claimed the children who went up in the flames would be granted ever-lasting life.

But I knew we must build our own future, in this life.

What other path can there be?

I heard these voices, crackling over the radios. And then they spoke of a ritual. It was being planned only a few hundred miles away. And all were welcome.

I went. I went to see if it was real.

I had to know.

It was real. I saw the horrors of Moloch. There were masses of people there. And I saw a crazy light in the eyes of many. I spoke to them. And I learned that they were the ones who had already given a child to the Dark King. I saw others filled with fear. Fear of what, I wasn't sure.

Then, I saw the sacrifices.

The first to go were not children. They were mostly men and women, although a few children were among them. I asked who they were, these sacrifices. One of the crazy-eyed men told me. They were heretics. They were resistors. They were not good enough for the fire.

They were not good enough to be lifted into the heavens as a smoke offering to the god of fire.

Instead, they would be stoned.

And they were.

Then I saw the children. There was a line of eight precious children. But their faces were not the faces of innocence. Yes, I could see their fear, but I could see something else. They were resolute, like I had been in as a child. They believed in Moloch and the everlasting gift of the fire. They had more certainty than even the parents who were offering them to the Dark King.

The children walked, one after another, into the fire. They screamed. They cried out. But they walked. And I could *smell* the burning of their flesh. As I watched, their parents were transformed. They went from mournful and frightened to joyous. I knew then that they *had* to be joyous. They had no other options. To accept that there was anything but joy in what they had done would be to destroy themselves for their decisions.

I asked one of the crazy-eyed men how the worship of Moloch had come to this place. He spoke of the prophecies that filled the airwaves. He spoke of a notebook, written by a prophet and brought by an apostle of that faraway man. The apostle had shared Moloch's anger at humanity, and his joy upon our sacrifices. That apostle spoke with such overwhelming belief. He had cried out in joy when he described his own sacrifice, and the freedom it had bought him. He described how a weight had been removed, knowing that he had dedicated all to Moloch.

Others had come to follow Moloch. He brought meaning and worth to what had been simple destruction. And, of course, the sun, poking even more through the thinning haze of smoke, demonstrated the blessings Moloch had offered.

I asked that crazy-eyed man what kind of G-d would demand the sacrifice of children. He began to cry out. He pointed at me. He shouted that I was a heretic.

I fled. I ran to my truck and I fled.

I fled back to SubTropolis. As I listened to the radio, I realized that the evil had surrounded us. I had seen it. It was real. It was coming close to our little collection of towns.

That was when I collected our radios, and I censored our communications. I throttled the supply of oil. No one could travel without my permission. No one could speak to the outside without *my* okay.

I believed in an open culture. I believed in the exchange of ideas. Nonetheless, I created a wall around my people.

And I preached. I travelled our communities preaching creation and life and children. I demanded that those around us embrace life. I demanded that my own people *represent* life. I even condemned my own actions and preferences. I knew *I* had to live an example. An example in which even the *symbolism* of squandered potential had to be resisted. An example in which life was held up in order to counteract a world that had been overcome by death.

Despite all I had done, Moloch came to us as surely as Darwin had come to me. The prophets of the Dark King could allow no other eventuality. They came to what used to be downtown Kansas City. They came to my domain. A woman ran from there. She fled to us. And she told us what was happening.

With our radios, we heard a new broadcast. From within our little domain. Moloch had infected my people.

Now, I'm standing outside the grid of old streets that used to be downtown. My men carry guns and gleaming, but chipped, machetes.

I, the lover of freedom and democracy and the open exchange of ideas, am about to condemn this little town. I am about to kill the men and women and even the rare children – because they have become the willing sacrifices to Moloch. These ideas cannot be allowed to survive.

I had expected to have second thoughts. I had expected to challenge my own decision. I had expected to awaken from the horror. But now I know that some ideas are necessary for the strength and development of a society. Just as the bacteria in the gut compete and evolve and thus eventually better serve the host, some ideas compete, providing the balance and the ideological conflicts that ultimately lead to a flourishing society. But some ideas are a cancer. They cannot be argued with. They cannot be integrated.

They must simply be destroyed.

That is why I am about to kill in the name of life.

My men look to me.

Just then, the old verses I learned as a child run through me.

Whosoever he be of the children of Israel, or of the strangers that sojourn in Israel, that giveth of his seed unto Molech; he shall

surely be put to death; the people of the land shall stone him with
stones. (Lev 18)

If there arise in the midst of thee a prophet, or a dreamer of
dreams--and he give thee a sign or a wonder, and the sign or the
wonder come to pass, whereof he spoke unto thee--saying: 'Let us go
after other gods, which thou hast not known, and let us serve them'...
that prophet, or that dreamer of dreams, shall be put to death... (Dev
13: 2-6)

If thou shalt hear tell concerning one of thy cities, which the
LORD thy G-d giveth thee to dwell there, saying: 'Certain base
fellows are gone out from the midst of thee, and have drawn away
the inhabitants of their city, saying: Let us go and serve other gods,
which ye have not known'; then shalt thou inquire, and make search,
and ask diligently; and, behold, if it be truth, and the thing certain,
that such abomination is wrought in the midst of thee; thou shalt
surely smite the inhabitants of that city with the edge of the sword,
destroying it utterly, and all that is therein and the cattle thereof,
with the edge of the sword. (Dev 13: 13-16)

I realize, in that instant, that I have become just like my parents.
How can I justify this? How can I embrace their darkness?

Then another verse comes to my mind.

See, I have set before thee this day life and good, and death and
evil, in that I command thee this day to love the LORD thy G-d, to
walk in His ways, and to keep His commandments and His statutes
and His ordinances; then thou shalt live and multiply, and the LORD
thy G-d shall bless thee in the land... (Dev 30)

I know, with certainty, that my people must survive.

I must stand for life, even if it means others must be condemned to death. I must kill so that the world does not succumb to the powers of Moloch.

My mind untroubled and my soul unburdened, I nod to my men.

I give them the order to proceed.

And I know that I am no longer a broken man.

In the Torah Reading of *RE'EH*, we read about the means the Torah uses to protect the people against incompatible ideals and symbolism. This story discusses those same ideas. In order to challenge both myself, and you, I chose to highlight the commandment to destroy the heretical city.

The question, of course, is what measures are justified *today,* in the world we currently live in, to protect the ideas of life and the preservation of potential. This story doesn't come packaged with answers, but perhaps it can raise a few questions.

Shoftim: Battle Dreams

I look around the truck's cabin, with its stark, harsh interior. I see the grim faces of the men. Below us, the armored personnel carrier is shaking violently as it moves through the rough terrain. The truck's wheels, suspension and frame seem to conduct the force of every pebble through to our spines. We're driving over a lot more than pebbles. The Armored Personnel Carrier (APC) has no windows and so we can't see anything. I do have a view of the battlefield, though. This isn't a normal APC. It is a mobile command post and in front of each of the men there is a bank of monitors, providing real-time information about the world around us.

Five minutes ago, the men had been the nexus of an effort to systematically take apart our enemy's military operations. Everything had been laid out years before. It was an awesome battle plan, and I was proud to have developed it. It was also classic. The enemy would attack and we would retreat under their assault. They would rush into the vacuum and we would surround them and eliminate their army. I would watch and manage everything from the back of the battlefield, off to the side of that central thrust, and well away from the enemy.

The enemy, somehow, noticed where my command vehicle was. They worked out my strategy. They only feinted down the middle, triggering our excessively eager retreat. My pincers moved into an encircling stance – turning all their efforts towards the central cavity. And then the enemy launched their primary assault. They attacked one side of the pincer, on its vulnerable edge.

Their assault moved remarkably quickly, rolling through a third of my army. Tanks, infantry and anti-missile units were caught unawares. Everything had turned in an instant. They were only minutes from my mobile command facility itself.

I had a choice then; I could have run, fleeing with my commanders and yielding to the enemy. Or I could turn and somehow try to hold off the assault.

I decided on the latter.

There was a ridge-line between us and the enemy. It wasn't much, but I thought that just maybe my small contingent of infantry, armor and anti-aircraft systems could hold it long enough to keep the enemy at bay. Maybe we could guide a response. My men, officers and analysts who were most comfortable behind a screen, were now rushing into combat.

It was dangerous, almost suicidal, but I really had no choice.

Now, I'm feeling every shock and vibration. The sounds of explosives are getting closer. Suddenly, the truck rocks violently to the left. It doesn't take much to realize a shell landed next to us and then exploded. The vehicle grinds to a halt. The driver calls out for orders; the truck is incapacitated. I made the call. I tell him to open the doors. He does and as a blast of hot and dust-filled air rushes into the APC, my men rise as one and run out the door. They are as smooth and efficient as the best-trained infantry. They move fearlessly into whatever fate has waiting for them.

I am right behind them.

I wonder, as I leap from the back of the truck, whether I have just built my entire life around a single terrible mistake.

I hadn't always been a military commander. I had, at one point, simply been a child. My father had been a Staff Sergeant in the Army; my mother a schoolteacher. I was their brilliant son. It was my brilliance that brought me into another world. Instead of hanging around with other children of the middle classes, I was thrust out of the world of my childhood. My academic acumen pushed me up and out. Soon I was surrounded by the children of tycoons, generals and members of Parliament.

All of them had things I did not have. They had wealth. They had glory. And they had power. All I had was brains. Brains and a desperate desire to fit in with the children of the elite.

My parents were jealous of the elites. They wanted what the elites had, and they wanted *me* to get it for them. They wanted me to get them what they could not get for themselves.

I saw things the same way my parents did. I wanted what the elite children had, and I didn't hide it. Those children would taunt me with stories of their parents' achievements and prides. I couldn't answer them with anything. I would sulk, angry and frustrated. And I would destroy them in the classroom, but they didn't care about that. My grades earned me no jealous resentment from my peers.

As I grew older, the national educational system recognized my unique capabilities. I was offered a coveted spot in a military academy. It was almost a unique offer. Half of my education would be at the military academy itself while the other half would be at the nation's best technical university. I would graduate a Lieutenant, but so much more was expected of me. I expected so much more of myself.

That was the first time others were jealous of me. It was subtle. A few of the children of the great ones were in my program. But they knew strings had been pulled for them to get there. They knew I was the one who *deserved* to be there. They were jealous. They were jealous and I loved it.

I piled it on from there on, glorying in every promotion and rubbing every success in their noses. My peers may have hated me, but my superior officers loved me. I did whatever I could to climb the ranks. Soon, my peers were not the sons of the great but the officers who had once commanded me. I had thrust myself forward and I reveled in my success.

Shortly after my 43rd birthday, I became the youngest commander of my nation's military.

But I had not yet acquired what the sons of the great had. I did not have wealth. I did not have glory. The only power I had was within the military itself.

That was why I conceived of this war.

We'd long had tensions with a neighboring country. I realized it would be simple enough to escalate those tensions. I'd be able to suck our neighbor into a war. I'd be able to stealthily undermine peace talks. I'd be able to make it look like *they* were the aggressor. They *were* a natural aggressor. Their army was larger than ours and they had a history of belligerence.

When they attacked, though, I knew I'd be able to outsmart them. I would rescue my people. We would have glory, power and wealth. I would make all three my own. Taking responsibility for the blessings my country had earned.

I'd worked for years on this plan. Now, though, it is all unraveling.

As we race out of the APC, the smoke chokes our lungs. Even though the visibility is almost zero, I can see the crater where the shell struck. A few feet over and we wouldn't have survived. It had been day when I'd set up the command post, but now it is night. I know the terrain. I've memorized every detail. I know where the ridgeline is. I call my men, over the din of low-flying aircraft, machine guns and high explosives. I call them and rally them – my little team of analysts and armchair soldiers. They follow me up that hill. And behind them I can hear the rumbling of our few remaining tracked vehicles: tanks, artillery and anti-aircraft hardware.

I can't retreat, though. People might discover what I had done, risking the country for my own honor. And they would circle on me and destroy me. My parents' position would have seemed elevated then.

We bunker down on the face of that ridge. I can see the enemy approaching. I ask a fellow officer for his laser designator. I watch the enemy. I don't want to fire, yet. They don't necessarily know we are here. But before long, I know which vehicles contain their commanders. I know which are scouts, designated to warn of our other pincer moving in from their side. And I know which form key parts of their attack formations. I use the designator to point them out one by one.

Then the artillery from across the battlefield begins to fire.

Even though the attack formations threaten us most directly, I designate the Commanders first. Then the scouts. Then the loci of their formations. I leave them for last because without the commanders and scouts, our enemy will be both confused and blind. They will not be able to resist us.

My calculations are correct. The enemy's advance falters. When the other side of my army turns and attacks, the enemy does not see them coming and soon turns into a disorganized jumble of a force.

In under an hour, it is over.

In under an hour, I have achieved everything I wanted. Not only have I won glory for my people, I served as a courageous key to the success of the battle.

I am wrapped in courage, glory, honor and respect.

I know I will be Prime Minister and my children will grow up wrapped in all the wealth, power and glory I did not have. I know that as time passes, my name will be on the lips of my country's schoolchildren. I gloat. For a time.

Then I hear the distant artillery again. Confused, it takes me a moment to realize somebody is knocking.

"Sir!" I hear a voice call. It is my Chief of Staff.

Still confused, I slowly tear apart the threads of my sleeping fantasy from those of reality. I am the child of a Sergeant and a teacher. I did climb the ranks and I have been picking a fight with a neighbor. All of that is real.

But the war has not yet come.

Today is the day of the critical negotiations. Today is a day I have long planned. Like Bismarck, I will draw my enemies into battle and then embarrass and destroy them.

Today is the linchpin of my life's strategy.

But, now, *something* is wrong.

I rise from my couch and fetch my cap.

I have work to do.

As I enter the negotiation room, my dream nags at me. If that shell had landed only a few feet over, I would have been forgotten and my enemies would have been honored.

The difference was not of my own making.

I would have taken all of those risks, and all of those lives would have been lost, and for what? The glory of my people?

I take my seat at the table. The others are already there. There are wealthy diplomats, there are glorious generals, and there are powerful ministers. These are the great men and women of both our peoples. And all of us are seeking honor and glory.

In reality, though, what we are doing is destroying each other – and then gloating over *our* portion of what remains.

Our Foreign Secretary is about to speak, but I cut him off.

"Let's exchange spies," I say.

Everyone looks at me, befuddled.

"You'll take my spies and put them in your border region. You will place my radars near your Air Force bases. And I'll do the same with your spies and your radars. And we'll both be pretty certain neither side is trying anything tricky."

"What about our dispute?" asks one of the enemy.

"None of our fundamental needs are incompatible. We can resolve our issues. Think about it, if we go to war, history may glorify the winners. The winners might claim the wealth of their enemies. They might claim power over them. But they won't have added anything to the world. They will just have shifted the cards between them. But with peace, think of the lives we can save, the hopes we can enable others to realize. To quote an ancient source, think of the vineyards to be planted, of the marriages to be established and of the houses to be built."

My own side looks at me, as if I've betrayed them. For their part, the enemy does not look satisfied. They too want the contest of war.

"We will respect your borders and you will respect ours. We will come to an agreement. But you must understand, if there must be war, it will not be driven by *our* quest for glory, money or power. It will be driven by yours. And we will teach the world the cost of such motivations. We will use you as an example. We will not be driven by circumstance, but by cold consistency. Our war will be a holy war, and you will be made an example of. You will be destroyed."

I see fear now, in their faces. If there is to be a war it will not be a war of glory, but a war of elimination. I also see satisfaction in the eyes of my own people. Finally, I see acceptance of my proposal growing among them all.

I know then that we in that room will not be wrapped in glory.

But we will come to a peace. Our actions will be woven, silently, into the future of our peoples.

The Torah reading of *SHOFTIM* features a stock speech for war. It basically says: "Don't be afraid, G-d is on your side." It seems odd for two reasons. First, it is a stock speech; it says nothing about the causes of a particular conflict. And second, how do you know G-d is on your side?

The answer comes earlier in the reading. We are told we can choose a King. A King is not simply a ruler. Any old dictator can have power. Only a King is honored. *It is an honor to serve a King.* When this reading tells us what kind of King to choose, we learn about the national values we should aspire to.

The naughty list includes the pursuit of horses (aka military glory), women and money. These pursuits guided the sons of the mighty (*BINAI ELOHIM*) before the flood. They corrupt mankind. Thankfully, the Torah leaves us with a contrary list. It includes brotherly love, self-control, humility and an awareness of G-d's commands. These are the national values we must honor.

But the reading does not stop there. We learn other keys to self-regulation. We learn of the priests and judges settling disputes. They

71

are the forces of conservatism. And we learn of the prophets providing Divine guidance; theirs are the voices of change. All their claims to power are overlapping, set up in opposition to each other. They represent a balance. We learn of the cities of refuge, which provide a damper to our bloodlust. The reward for these cities is more such cities. This is how we grow as a people. We learn that we must respect our neighbor's borders, as defined *prior* to entering the land. The family borders are not established – *this* concept is tribal and national in character. And then we learn of the stock speech for war and the concept of total wars of annihilation in which only trees are spared.

Only a nation that does not serve glory, that controls its own passions, that is open to the guidance of G-d and that respects the borders of its neighbors may practice this form of war. In fact, when an enemy has no justification for attack (think Nazi Germany against the United States), the response has a moral objective. A lesson was being made of the German cities when they were carpet-bombed cities at the end of the war. The lesson was that not only the military was guilty of the sins of the nation; the nation itself had to bear the cost of being seduced by such evil. But even in the case of such a terrible war, we preserve the trees – we preserve the legacies of those who came before the current generation of zero-sum antagonists.

The Torah portion brings it all together in the end with the case of unsolved murder. We are a people that preserves life and potential above all else. When a life is lost and the killer is not punished, we must nationally atone for our failure. To do this, we cut the back of the neck of a heifer (*EGLA*). The calf represents our prideful selves, as seen with the sin of the Calf. By cutting the neck, a symbol of our stiff-necked pride, we recognize we have no claim to pride if our land is a land of destruction and not of creation.

The path to glory starts with a chip on one's shoulder. Not long ago, Israel was – just like the commander in this story – surrounded by nations that could lay claim to power, money and glory. The Jewish people themselves had none of the above. We wanted to fit in with the elite, and we had the talents necessary to compete. We have done admirably. But we must always remember our past. In our past, we have pursued glory and power. It earned us nothing but brief spasms of honor. Now, we have aged. We have had an opportunity to internalize the lessons of this reading. While we must defend ourselves, we must also remember that it is not an honor to serve the glory, wealth or power of our nation. Our honor comes from far greater ambitions.

If we practice the values that run through this reading, our example can spread throughout the world and forever undermine the spirit of glory-seeking corruption that threaten the human race.

Ki-Tetzei: Deut 23:19

My father's body is sprawled out on his office floor. His head has been torn apart by a single bullet. The gun is still in his hand.

My father has just taken his own life. The only explanation, the only note, is a reference to a verse. "Deut 23:19."

I have long hated my father. I have long despised his weakness. Now, though? Now, I am simply confused. He was a man who gave up so much. A man who surrendered in the face of every challenge. He defended nothing he believed in. And now, he has killed himself over an obscure Bible verse: Deut 23:19.

"Thou shalt not bring the hire of a harlot, or the price of a dog, into the house of the LORD thy G-d for any vow; for even both these are an abomination unto the LORD thy G-d."

What kind of coward fails to fight for his beliefs, time after time, only to die defending a principle as tangential as this?

Why die for Deut 23:19?

Even as I ask the question, I know what must come next. I take the note to the kitchen. I burn it on the stove. And then, and only then, I call the police.

Perhaps I too am a coward.

My father was a preacher and I grew up in his church. 'Preacher' might not the right word. He had a small church in which all were welcome. The thing is, he did *almost* everything you'd expect in a church. The most constant of activities was the hosting of meals. Not for the hungry, per se, just for people. Any kind of people. He struggled mightily, but he brought people into his church. Then he fed them. The unusual thing was what he didn't do. Despite ample opportunities, he never, ever, preached.

I didn't understand him or what he was doing. I'd read about churches. We learned about them in school. The teachers always cast a disdainful eye in my direction, as they explained the evils of the past to the students in class. Churches were technically legal, but very few remained. The ideas they had once held onto were seen as immoral. Those old ideas were condemned and those who persisted in holding on to them were themselves condemned. They were paraded on camera. They were interviewed and mocked and ripped apart – publicly. Then they were banished. Nobody would do business with them, nobody would rent them a place to stay, no governments would serve them and nobody would sell them food – much less feed them. Those who grasped such incompatible beliefs were pariahs; modern man knew better than to accept their medieval views.

But my father had a church. It was a single large room. There was everything from a kitchen to a coat cupboard in that one open space. Only the bathroom and my father's small office were walled off. I grew up in that church. My bed was a cot we placed in the middle of the floor at night.

At first, I thought my father didn't believe in the old ideas. After all, he never preached. But, as I grew older, he began to teach. Not his hundreds of congregants, but me alone. He began to teach me what he believed. And he began to teach me why. As I learned, I realized that he was entirely at odds with the world around him. But I also saw that he defended nothing he believed in. He just ran his little church, feeding whoever would come, but telling them nothing of what he truly believed.

He just watched the world go by. He never had the strength to resist it. He ran a soup kitchen for those who needed no soup.

As I learned, I realized my mother had been the same. She too had never preached. But she too was a true believer. She too had given up her life for her beliefs. My mother had been identified as a cancer risk when she was still a young woman. A DNA patch was available. She turned it down. She refused it because it would change the core of who she was. When the time came, she was denied any treatment whatsoever. She had rejected the State, and the State rejected her. She had chosen a mysterious and cruel G-d over a little update to her genetic code. They would let her die with the consequences of her choice. Like my father, she gave up her life, but achieved nothing.

Now, because of a single obscure verse, I have no parents.

The police come, eventually. Police are rare in our world. There is rarely cause for their intervention. Murder and robbery are almost unheard of. Suicide is even rarer. With DNA patches, mental illness and depression have largely been cured. Naturally, the police have evolved. They no longer see their primary role as the prevention of physical crime. They see it as the prevention of ideological crime. I know, as they come through the door of our tiny church, that they won't be seeking to investigate a possible murder.

Instead, with the death of so rare a churchman, they will seek something more fundamental.

The police do not cuff me. There is no need to. They just inform me that I am under arrest. I want to scream and shout and fight back. But there is a reason there are no cuffs. Resistance would accomplish nothing. I am just one young man caught up in currents far beyond my own power to control.

Everything began to change generations ago. It all started when we began to learn how to manipulate DNA. It started slowly, but then accelerated exponentially. The greatest change came in 2015, with the creation of CRISPR, a DNA manipulation kit. All around the world, people began to hack DNA. And before long, the fabric of our world was changed. Parents no longer conceived a child, they designed them around their own values. They put their thumb on the scales of intelligence and beauty and strength. And they chose what they cared about. It was seen as purer than 'random' humanity. It was about ideas, not the weakness of chance. Researchers using CRIPR and far more advanced, later, tools, poured their efforts into identifying tradeoffs they could eliminate. They were, and are, always seeking a child who can be more beautiful *and* more intelligent. And, they have succeeded.

While there are variations in degree, human children of my generation are universally attractive and smart and physically fit. But they are not unique. They are produced in genetic batches, like cars. Only small changes to their paint jobs distinguish them from their peers.

I stick out from my peers. I am not as intelligent as most. In conversation, they can detect it. More obviously, I am *ugly*. People may not place all the weight of their thumbs on the scale of beauty, but they rarely abandon it altogether. My parents did not tip the genetic scale. I am not only fat, I have close-set eyes, a broad and flat nose, acne and basically no chin. People never notice my blue eyes or brown hair. It is far easier to describe me as 'the ugly one.'

I stick out, a mute testimony to the hidden beliefs of my parents.

Of course, the tweaking of humanity was only the first part of our genetic manipulation. New *kinds* of people have been created. We created Judges. They combine brilliance with selfless dedication to the law. They are not machines; the law is inherently gray. But human corruption has been taken from them. There are Workers of every kind, cleaning the streets and homes, repairing infrastructure and growing crops. Strength and stamina define them. But they serve humanity. And there are, of course, the Companions. They are not dedicated to the service of law or humanity as a whole, but to the love of their caretakers. They combine the intelligence and anatomy of humans with the loyalty of dogs.

As the years have passed, more and more of these manipulations have appeared. Our economy has rewarded innovators and innovation has accelerated. Human children exist, but increasingly even they are rare. Why have a child, who may or may not obey, when you can have a child-Companion who will always be loyal to you?

Now, instead of families there are human-Companion pairs with Companion children. The Companions can be legally married, with the marriages recognized by the State. There was some resistance to this, at first. But it was snuffed out. After all, who would want to deny people validation and love and respect? Who would want to deny the selfless Companions the same. Must they live lives without fulfillment simply because of antiquated ideas of marriage?

For his part, my father abhorred it all. He would quietly read to me from the Bible, verbally highlighting the texts that rejected our reality.

He abhorred it all, but he did nothing to combat it.

The police station is a pleasant place. The ceilings are high and the room is well lit. There is no threat in the air. There are no cursing criminals, cages or cells. There is nowhere to run, after all. In a world

78

of loyal servants and swift and fair judges, there is nowhere to hide and no reason to hold the guilty. Justice can be delivered swiftly, once the truth is uncovered.

Instead of barriers and walls, there are just a few open desks, with police detectives – Servants all – sitting patiently at them.

I am brought to one of them. I guess she has been assigned my father's death. She is, not surprisingly, a strikingly beautiful Servant. Humans are known to yield more easily to physically beautiful people. Had I been a child, the Servant would have been matronly. Had I been interested in men; a male Servant would have been chosen. Everything has been designed to get my cooperation with a minimum of struggle.

The detective asks me questions. I find myself acting just as my father had. I am pleasant and agreeable, but I shed no light on my father's death. She'll have to work it out for herself.

I know it won't take her long, though.

It also won't take long for the punishment to be delivered.

I am placed in an apartment. There is no outgoing network access here and there are no phones. The point is not punishment, but separation. I might have dangerous ideas and they can't allow them to spread. My communications must be controlled. The apartment is pleasant. It is well-stocked and well appointed. Prisoners live well. They live better, actually, than I had with my parents.

My mother had been a doctor, but not a popular one. Her patients were drawn from the continually dwindling number who rejected genetic treatments. Even before she died, we'd struggled with money. The church business, in a world without churches, is not a profitable work. It didn't help that my father sunk everything he had into those meaningless meals.

The apartment is nice, so I decide to enjoy it while I can.

The man had been a regular at the church. His name was Andrew Bright. He was a researcher – human, not Servant. He had been tremendously successful man, before coming to my father's meals. His designs had provided the basis for hundreds of thousands of Companions and Companion-children worldwide. He had made a fortune in his business. He was also a very public person, constantly praising the value of Companions and the validation they offered. He was a poster-child of modern values.

It surprised me when my father welcomed him to the Church. After all, we'd often talked about the evils of Andrew Bright and his ilk. As my father had explained it, Andrew Bright had ripped apart the fabric of human life itself.

My father's challenge was easy enough to understand. Human relationships are fraught with work and risk and danger. They are filled with unpredictability and disloyalty. They are condemned by judgment. But Companion relationships are pure and trustworthy and giving. So, humans do not relate to other humans. They are never challenged in their decisions. Instead, they just stay in their own homes. Goods are delivered to them by some types of Servants. Entertainment is created for them by other types. Validation and love are always close at hand. No matter their own imperfections or limitations or choices, they are free of criticism. Why would they seek out the challenge of human relations when they live as atomic units, disconnected from the world around them and surrounded only by the praise of angels.

Andrew Bright may not have created this problem, but he did a great deal to advance it.

Still my father welcomed him; just as he had welcomed dozens of his Companion creations.

With time, Andrew became a regular. Then he came to my father, in his tiny office, and offered him a gift. It was a substantial gift, enough to run the church for a lifetime. I saw my father's face then, the conflict in his eyes. Andrew, of course, could not detect it.

My father told Andrew, then and there, that he would get back to him in a few days. That had been the beginning of the end.

As I sit in the prison apartment, watching some meaningless show on a screen in my bedroom, I can already envision the cameras and the hot lights making me sweat. I can already envision the questions. They'll be broadcasting it globally, as they have before. It is a modern inquisition. I will be made to confess to the world. With that, they'll be condemning me and my father and everything we believe in. After all, humans do not validate those who question their most questionable decisions.

I know how it will go. I'll be typecast as a 'random'; a throwback to an era before proper human design. I'll be typecast as a religious nut, with a suicidal preacher of a father, and a mother who preferred to die than manipulate her own DNA. I'll be typecast and then they'll strike at what *I* believe, mocking my rejection of modernity. I can see it, and there is nothing I can do to stop it from happening. I cannot be honest and avoid becoming their exhibit.

I know I'll do what others have done. I'll rail against them. I'll try to explain to humanity what they're missing; the challenges G-d has placed before us that we simply sidestep with our technology. I'll try to argue that sitting at home being loved and entertained is not *true* fulfillment. I will be mocked, and I will achieve nothing. I will achieve less than nothing. Because all I will accomplish is the further consolidation of their crushing ideological front.

But I don't know what else to do.

In the three days that followed Andrew Bright's offer, my father knelt in prayer at the front of our church. He ate and drank nothing, although I continued to host our meals. The guests would look in confusion at the man kneeling at the foot of the unused dais. I was also confused. My father had been willing to accept so much, even though he rejected these 'families' in his heart, they never saw it. I knew him better than any other person and I never saw him show any sign of disdain for the guests at our table.

And yet, Mr. Bright's genuine generosity and appreciation seemed to have brought him low.

I watched him pray and I imagined that he was seeking some sort of guidance.

On the third day, he rose weakly to his feet. There were no guests then. I was cleaning in the kitchen. I watched him go. A minute later, I heard the report of the gun.

My father had found his answer. But I still didn't understand the question. Yes, Mr. Bright made his money selling Companions and Companion children. He rented prostitutes and sold dogs – substitute relationships. His livelihood was abhorrent: Deut 23:19.

This was why my father could not take his money.

That much was obvious. But why had *this* driven him to suicide. Why had he decided to die on *this* hill, and none of the others?

I am summoned to another interview. Hardly an hour has passed. There are cameras here, ready to capture footage for my eventual global shaming. The detective across from me already understands what drove my father to his own death. The only question she'll have is whether I too am a danger to society.

I sit at her desk, physically comfortable but wracked with uncertainty. Do I make my stand here? Spitting helplessly in the face of a bureaucrat who has committed no sin of her own? She is, after all, simply a Servant – she is not responsible for the essence of her being. Do I waste myself here and then vanish into obscurity – or worse, into the maw of universal condemnation?

Or do I lie? Do I tell her I have rejected my parents, both of them, entirely. They might let me go. I might reenter society. They'll monitor me, to be sure. But they won't think I'm a threat simply because I won't be one. Perhaps I could get a Companion of my own, and simply disappear into a safe obscurity.

Wasn't this what my father would have done?

As soon as I ask the question of myself, I am leveled by a flash of insight. I know that this is *not* what my father did.

"Joshua?" asks the detective, in her sweet and pleasant voice, "Do you know why your father killed himself?"

I nod.

"Can you tell me?" she asks.

"He could not accept a gift from a man who sold companions. He killed himself for even considering the offer."

She nods, politely.

"And how do you feel about his decision?"

I give her the first answer that comes to mind. "He shouldn't have given up his life for something so trivial."

She nods again.

I find myself asking, in that moment, was it actually so meaningless? After all, my father was not a stupid man.

"I meant," she continues, "Do you agree with his decision to reject Mr. Bright's offer?"

I think for a moment. The Bible had commanded it. But the Bible commanded many things my father ignored. Why had he died for this?

Perhaps it was just a step too far. He had spent his life being boiled slowly. He spent his life retreating. But at some point, perhaps, he had drawn a line. He had decided he could not take that which was abhorrent, and dedicate it to the service of G-d. His church could not be funded by prostitutes and dogs. The other decisions were society's responsibility. But this one was his. It was something small, but reality is built on small decisions.

I decide to lie. I don't understand enough, not yet, to give everything up for this point alone.

"No," I say, "I don't agree. He should have accepted Mr. Bright's money."

The detective just nods. It is clear she doesn't quite believe me. But despite all of our genetic advancements, we still can't tell – for sure – when somebody is lying.

Her question continues to nag at me, though.

Was this *all* my father had done? Had everything else actually been surrender?

The detective continues: "Has your father sacrificed in other ways for his antiquated beliefs?"

"No," I say. I believe it, for just that instant.

Then, almost as quickly, I realize that it isn't true. My father lost his wife. My parents were always poor. He dedicated himself to sharing meals with creatures he abhorred. And he was silent for his entire life.

He sacrificed for his beliefs in a million little ways.

But he didn't fight back, did he? He just suffered silently for a cause only he believed in.

"Why did your father feed so many at his church?"

I don't know the answer to this question. I'd never asked it. I'd prepared what felt like tens of thousands of meals and I'd never asked why we'd done it.

I think about the question. But I don't even know enough to lie.

Deep down, a realization begins to gnaw at me. The meals were the core of everything.

Then, I see it. He brought people together so some kernel of humanity could understand the value of *human* relationships. He drew them out of their apartments and homes so they could experience something different. If he had rejected them, nothing would have been achieved. But, perhaps, they could accept his loyalty. Not the blind loyalty of a Companion to a human caretaker; but the complex loyalty of a human to his G-d. Perhaps by giving them the experience of that loyalty, he could begin to change humankind.

"He liked people," I say, simply. The detective nods. It is hard to argue with liking people. It isn't a crime. And the answer is entirely truthful. Of course, my father's own success destroyed him. He converted Andrew Bright, in his way.

"Are Companions abhorrent to your G-d?"

I know the answer to this question. Or, at least, I know the answer I will give. I will lie to this detective, as my father lied to everyone but me. Then I will continue what he started, offering meals to all who wish to come. I will offer them the challenges and risks and great rewards, of human relationships.

I will never speak of what I truly believe.

I will lie, and I will be free. Then, perhaps I too will marry a human woman, have an ugly child and a church. A church in which I will never preach.

Instead, my family and my life will serve as an example. I will preach in silence, just as my father had done.

"Do you reject Companion marriage?"

I am speaking easily now, giving her the answers she wants. This is ground I can surrender.

In my mind, though, I ask: 'what if Andrew Bright offers me his money? What will I do then?'

I sit there, lying pleasantly to the detective. She drones on, trying to find a trace of heresy. But I know her beliefs, the world knows her values. They are easy enough to ape.

Even as I lie, my appreciation for the man my father had been just grows and grows. Then I know what I will do with Mr. Bright. If he makes the same offer to me, I will take a risk. I will explain, privately, that his money is not welcome. If my father's greatest convert turns on me, I will know that there is no hope.

Perhaps, though, just maybe, Mr. Bright will give me his most valuable gift: his silence.

As the patrolmen walk me from the station, I emerge absolved of all charges. And I know, then, that my father was no coward. He was simply a man who chose his battlefields carefully. His own caution drove him to suicide – he betrayed more than he could accept. But he was no coward.

As I emerge into the sunlight beyond the station doors, I realize my father's truth: it is through the small things that the world is reinvented.

This week's Torah portion is a collection of small laws. Placed in the context of the Pinocchio nation – brought to life through Moshe's great speech – it seems like an odd reading. Some classify it as a simply a collection of laws that had no prior place. To me, at least, it has a clear purpose and role. The other readings spoke of great trends and goals and values. They spoke of our national immune system and self-control and responsibility and love of G-d. But none of that is real without the *little* things. None of that is real without the tiny practical building blocks that define the relationship between humans and between humankind and G-d.

The first part of the reading focuses on laws of neighborly consideration (which includes respecting G-d's role in the definition of species). The second on preserving reality in relationships (which is where the dogs and prostitutes come in). The third on defending the spark of our humanity (with limits on punishment). The final section focuses on fighting back against the breakdown of human consideration (honest weights).

Together, these sections speak to the little things.

The book of DEVARIM is about creating a nation, a living, breathing, nation with a heart to know, eyes to see and ears to hear. The great values that describe such a nation might motivate it. But it is these small practical laws that hold it together. It is these laws that enable the body of the nation to form.

After all, our lives are rarely defined by a constant pursuit of the highest moral visions. Instead, we build on small things. We build on routines: conversations with parents, groceries for kids and even meals shared with the communities around us.

It is only on the basis of these small things that we can pursue our greatest objectives.

p.s. Yes, we have a dog. And six children.

Ki-Tavo: The Story of Hassan

I've never had such fear before. I've had fear – the most primal and fundamental kind of fear.

But it was nothing like this.

--

It is the morning of May 28, 2010. I wake up to the savory smell of chole and freshly-baked kulche wafting through our room. My wife is a skilled cook. With her chole, she brings chickpeas together with a mix of spices and a touch of tomato and something fantastic emerges. Her kulche is also fantastic. She bakes the flat-rolled flour dough in a clay oven – one she made – until it is golden brown and perfectly fluffy. The whole neighborhood claims she makes the best kulche in Pakistan. They may be right.

I know, if I try hard enough, that I can detect a more subtle odor, the odor of the chaas she makes. To make it, she combines salted yogurt, cumin and freshly ground ginger in the right proportions. Chaas is normally refreshing, but she makes it something transformative. Its scents lightly float over the others, barely detectable, but filling the whole picture in. When I drink her chaas, I can close my eyes and imagine myself someplace perfect. The effect is somehow even more remarkable when I am already in that perfect place, with her.

As I wake up, these are the smells that bathe my soul. Our walls are infused with the scents of ginger and cumin and cardamom and anise and nutmeg and cloves. Our home is tiny – a dilapidated shack in a small slum in north Lahore, Pakistan. But in this regard, its size is an advantage. Every surface exudes flavor. I've been to bigger homes, much bigger homes. But the flavors of those homes are restricted. They are locked in. Often, they are barely detectable even in the kitchen itself. The rest of the house is dead. But not our shack. Our shack is thoroughly filled with life and with love. We've been trying for years to add more life and more love to it – but without success. Somehow, we've been able to hold on to the other joys in our lives.

The smells of chole, kulche and chaas are normal, but I don't normally wake up to them. Normally I wake up very early in the morning – even before my wife – and head to the mosque for the first prayer. Of course, we can't call it a mosque – to do so would bring prison. Our 'place of prayer' stands tucked behind a Shell gas station. It is set back at an angle. In front of it is a broad boulevard with trees that run down its center.

After prayers, I walk another 500 meters to my work in the famous Mayo Gardens. The Gardens form a complex of over 70 massive homes on beautiful, tree-filled, estates. They were originally built for high-ranking officers serving on the British-Indian railway. Now, colonels, generals and the like live there. The place is walled, gated and patrolled. You need special ID to enter. Because of my religion, I can't get a passport or a national ID – but I can still get the special ID I need to work in the Mayo Gardens. It is part of the disorder of my homeland. My job is to maintain the houses. I can repair air conditioners, fix ancient electrical wiring and repair plumbing. I can repair walls, roofs and floors. I don't install new things though. I just keep ancient things alive. There's a lot of demand for that in Pakistan.

I love the Mayo Gardens; you enter and you are hidden from the din of traffic and the grime of the city. It is like you enter an entirely different universe. I've always loved this part of the city – where a few artificial lines separate my slum, which is so tightly packed there aren't even streets, from some of the most stunning homes in the country. I imagine they are among the most stunning homes in the world.

But this morning isn't a normal morning. I'm not rushing to early prayers and then work. This is a Friday morning. I don't work on Fridays. On Fridays, I wake up to the smells of my wife's cooking and I spend my day with her before going to the 'place of prayer'.

Hina and I met when I was 7 and she was 6. People are fond of arranged marriages in my part of the world. But we met so young, and were so clearly matched, that our parents agreed that we'd marry one another. We had no choice, but we didn't want one. We like to joke that we alone have a love-arranged marriage. We actually married when I was 18, moving into our little shack and filling it with the scents of our lives.

I get out of bed and look across the room. Hina is pulling the kulche from the clay oven. It looks beautiful, as does she. Behind her, on our small bench, are a few mangoes. But there is something else, on our small propane stove, something I somehow missed. There is kheer, a rice pudding flavored with cardamom, saffron and almonds. This is an unusual treat.

We eat breakfast. I tell her about the Gardens. I do it every week. She can't go there, she doesn't have my special ID. Still, she loves to hear about everything from which trees are flowering to the petty problems of the powerful. This week is no different – if anything she seems more engaged and I feel even happier to share. Hina works as well. She cooks. Half the neighborhood seems to be sustained by her food. She tells me about the lives of our neighbors. Despite living in a

91

slum, we do well. We have the money to move someplace with streets – but we have no desire to do so.

We are Ahmadi – Muslims who believe that the Madhi, or Messiah, has come. You could call us the Mosque of the Latter Day Prophets. We believe it is our job to repair the relationship between man and Allah by bringing out the Divine in mankind. We believe it is our role to end religious conflict – by holding ourselves out as an example of peaceful dedication. Our method is not the most popular one. Because we believe there was a prophet after Mohammed, there are laws against us. We aren't allowed to call ourselves Muslim, publicly quote from the Koran or pray with other Muslims. Just quoting from the Koran can land us in prison – and occasionally much worse. Our Kalif fled, decades ago, to London.

The government calls us Qadiani – from the town we came from in India. It is intended as an epithet.

Our religious rituals are the same as the rest of Pakistan's. We also accept the Five Pillars as they do. Nonetheless, our practice is dramatically different. We have returned to the true meaning of Islam. Islam means 'peace' and we are pacifists. We do not protest or scream in the streets. We do not attack those who disagree with us – even if they insult us and our religion. Instead, we fight evil by offering praise to Allah and Mohammed his prophet. In light of the threats against us, our Kalif has recommended only that we pray.

And so, after sharing our weekly experiences, Hina and I discuss the news. We start with the blasphemy cases against our people, we move on to the threats. And then we talk about the politics of Pakistan – the broader currents through which we swim. The conversation will continue at the mosque – Friday services are an opportunity to work through community issues. But Hina won't be there.

One thing we never talk about is children. There is never anything new to share.

After we talk, I use a rag to bathe myself. I put on my best clothes and I leave the house for the mosque.

Today, though, something is different. Hina also gets changed. And we leave the house together.

We walk between the warren of tightly packed shacks until we get to the edge of the slum. And then we walk down the street to the mosque itself. The men are streaming into it. Very few women are there, just passerby. A few volunteer guards, not Ahmadi, stand outside. We walk to the edge of the gas station and we stop. A collection of motorbikes and delivery trucks charge down the boulevard.

Just as I am about to leave her, she touches my arm – gently. "Hassan," she says, "One more thing."

"Yes?" I ask. There is a ding as a car enters the gas station.

"I'm pregnant." She says. Just like that.

I'm stunned. I stand there, stunned.

And then she smiles a deep and complete smile. "Go in," she says, "You're late."

I walk towards the mosque. I look back just as I come to the door. She is standing there, watching.

She smiles and waves.

And then there is a clink, a few shouts and an explosion.

And she is no longer there.

--

The attack lasted two and a half hours. The police came, but they just watched. We are Ahmadi, they would not risk their lives for us. And, of course, we did not fight. Instead, the killers went through the

93

main prayer hall and killed everyone. They had time to double-check their murders. One of them ascended our orange-tinted minaret, its view enabled him to shoot any who tried to escape. Between our two main mosques, 89 people were killed that day. Over two and half hours of fear.

In the end, the attackers blew themselves up – spreading yet more death.

They are the antithesis of us.

I remember hiding in an office, under a desk, and praying. But other than that, I remember almost nothing from that day. Just the first clink, the initial shouts and the explosion that killed my wife.

She was the only woman killed that day. 88 men and one woman – my wife. My wife who had come to the mosque to share the best news of our lives.

I returned to our shack that that night. The scents were still there, but already they had begun to fade.

After that, my life became daily travels from home to mosque to work and back to home. I bought my food from a cart. There was no one to share my stories with. There was just a fading scent.

Others tried to get me to marry again. But I refused. Hina had always been the only one for me. And we'd shared so much together. Nobody could be permitted to erase her memory.

Four years later, the last lingering scents are almost gone.

--

It is a typical summer day when I walk to mosque. The rain is pouring down as the monsoon pummels the city. The mud in the slum is loosening up. Gutters in the streets are running over. It is punishingly hot. I walk to mosque – not in my finest clothes, but in my other clothes. A thin shirt and light pants – totally soaked through. Normally, there are more guards than before. But they are mostly volunteers and the rain is coming down heavy today, so most of the guards haven't shown up. A man with a rifle is set up in the minaret. It is a position that can't be ceded again.

Of course, none of the guards are Ahmadi – we don't fight. We depend on Allah to be vengeful on our behalf. We must be an example of another path.

I nod at the guards and slip into the mosque. The men from the area have all collected. There is a vigorous conversation. I don't talk much, not anymore. But I listen. So, I approach the edges of the group – wondering whether yet another Ahmadi person has been assaulted or killed.

Instead, they are talking about a city. A city of refuge in the Israeli Golan where all religions and people are welcome. A city whose governing ethos is a cycle of productivity and connection to G-d. A city we would be at home in. The men are wondering whether anybody will go there. Whether any Ahmadi, sick of the persecution in Pakistan, would venture to this new place.

As they talk, a vision fills my head. I smell Hina's spices again. But not in my shack. I smell them in that place. I smell them filling it with joy and life and flavor.

I raise my hand to speak.

"Yes?" asks the Imam. Faces turn to me, surprised.

"I'll go." I announce.

"Excuse me?" asks the Imam.

"I'll go to this place," I repeat, "I'll move there."

"Were you listening?" asks the Imam, "We were just talking about how expensive it would be to get there."

"I'll open a stall there, in the market. I'll sell our spices. Punjabi spices. And you will all own a part of my stall. And when it makes money, I'll send it back here – so more of you can come."

"Punjabi spices?" asks another man, incredulously, "Why would a bunch of Arabs want Punjabi spices?"

"For the joy," I say, with complete conviction, "For the joy that they bring. They don't have to love them much though – I'll have one stall. There will be hundreds of thousands of people there. Nobody else will be selling Punjabi spices."

The crowd murmurs its analysis.

"Where will you get the spices?" asks another man.

"From you," I answer, "You will source them here and get them to me there."

More analysis.

"You are a very competent man," says yet another man, "And we know you are trustworthy."

It is a statement of fact, not of action.

"Where will you get the money?" interjects somebody else.

"I don't know." I answer.

There is a pause. The Imam speaks, "I know where he'll get the money. He'll get the money from us. We can start another Community there. Many there will be running from violent perverters of Islam. But he will be there to establish a purer voice. It will be a deed to be honored by Allah and he will bring praise to Mohammed. Allah will smile on those who give. Who here is ready to receive the blessings of Allah?"

One by one, the men raise their hands. Every one of them contributes something. The porters, the tuk-tuk drivers, the street cleaners, the men without jobs. Everyone contributes something.

They dedicate sums I know they can barely afford. It comes, in all, to 693,954 Pakistani Rupees. It is about $7,000 dollars. But it will take time to make their dedications real. Some have money. But for many, they must sell prized possessions to fulfill their pledges.

As I wait, I work with the Imam to figure out how I will get to the City. I have no passport and Pakistan won't grant me one. I am also a member of a sect hated in my homeland and in every country that lays along my route.

Finally, after three weeks, the money is collected. Some of it is cash, but most is gold – the universal currency. 18 grams of gold – in all an amount of gold about the size of a large olive. We pound it into 10th of a gram pieces. Gold is remarkably malleable. One olive can be cut into 180 pieces. The gold is sewn into my clothes. Finally, I am set on my way.

My mission is to preserve these pieces of gold so that I can pave a path for the others to follow me.

I travel to Karachi and board a fishing boat owned by an Ahmadi. The boat makes an unscheduled stop near Dubai. Another Ahmadi, from Saudi Arabia, meets me there. He takes me across the border and connects me to friends who take me to a town near Jordan called Turaif.

Every step costs money. Every step cuts into my olive of gold.

From there, Bedouin smugglers take me across the border to Jordan and then across the desert to the edge of Syria. Coming from the lushness of Pakistan, the Jordanian desert seems like a moonscape. There are no people. There is nothing I can see which is alive. There are a few desert tracks – but there are no roads and no towns. I promise the Bedouin future business if they treat me well –

and somehow, they believe me. I think they can tell how little I'd be worth in ransom.

I walk across the border into Syria. Few people are travelling in that direction. I'm in the south – areas controlled by the government and by non-ISIS opposition. The risk is not extreme. So, I walk and hitch rides through the ruins of that country until I finally come to the abandoned city of Qunietra.

Between bribes and extra fees, I show up at the doors of the City with only nine of my tiny pieces of gold remaining. They are worth about $320.

Thankfully, I don't have to wait long for my interview. The City intake officers bring me in almost immediately – I'm the first man who has come from Pakistan. In my broken English, I tell my story. They accept me.

I am glad to be here – to be in the City. But I have a problem. My nine pieces of gold have to build something – something my community is depending on. Nine pieces of gold isn't enough money for my stall.

****

I convert my nine pieces of gold to the local currency, the Zuz. My gold is worth 1274 Zuz. The Zuz are not physical cash – they are in an account I can access using my phone. There are benefits to this set up. When I spend my initial money each month – it is supplemented automatically, with each transaction. It is a progressive sales tax that actively helps the poor. If I am willing to be extremely thrifty, my Zuz can go further. But no matter how thrifty I am, I don't have enough money to order spices.

I expect to need a loan. The great western charities emphasize loans in places like Pakistan - microloans. But I don't want a loan. As a Muslim, they are forbidden – but reality sometimes makes them necessary. Gladly, I learn that loans are not available in the City. The government will not enforce their terms. It believes that loans focus on the downside of the world. They depend on and create great risks. I agree.

Thankfully, there is another road. There are investors. I book an appointment. And then I come to the trailer that serves as City Hall. They sit me in front of a computer and ask me to present my business to a group of unseen people on the other end of the line. They are from Europe and the United States. It is incredibly nerve wracking. I am not a speaker. Nonetheless, I must convince these people to buy a part of my business.

I do what I can. I tell them my story. I tell them Hina's story. I tell them what I want to share and what I want to achieve. And, remarkably, they invest. They invest 40,000 Zuz for 20% of my stall. 28,000 actually arrive in my business account. There is a cash flow tax of 12,000. I am worried at first, very worried. But it is explained to me that the tax will be reimbursed for whatever I spend on business expenses. The City wants to tax funds that aren't used to support basic life or productive business activity. They don't want to tax productive activity – as the taxing of anything tends to reduce its quantity.

So, I call the Imam and I order spices. They have to be shipped to Cyprus and then Israel – nobody can ship from Pakistan to the Zionist state itself. I spend 30,000 Zuz. Because of the refund, only 21,000 leaves my business account. I have the 1274 Zuz in my personal account, but it isn't mine – it belongs to my community. So, I work, as a handyman repairing brand-new things, and pay my wages into the business account until I've made it whole. In the meantime, I spend as little as I can – I need to preserve my funds. I live in the tent I received at the city gates. I stay in my allocated camp site. I buy a camp stove and a fry pan to cook my meals. One woman is renting out the use of her kiln. In the evenings, I make myself a small clay oven. Just like Hina's. I make myself a plate and a bowl to eat from. But I don't stop there, I make bowls to sell my spices from; bowls filled with deep streaks of color. They remain empty, in my tent, for now. And, of course, I buy food. I go to the nearly empty shuk, and I buy flour and chickpeas and other basics. I buy only what I need to live on. My food is unbelievably bland.

43 days later, after I pay another 5,000 Zuz in handling expenses to the port of Haifa and the shipper (thankfully, only 3,500 are deducted from my shrinking balance) the spices arrive. I buy a carpet.

Early in the morning, right after the first prayer, I carry all my belongings to the shuk. I set up my tent as a windbreak and I lay my carpet out as a floor. I put down the bowls and I fill them with my spices.

And then I sit behind them and wait.

As I sit in my stall. I watch the people go by. They go where I went. To buy the necessities of life. None stop for the foreign luxury of Punjabi spices.

And then an overwhelming fear overcomes me. I fear, suddenly, that Arabs will not buy Punjabi spices. I fear that all the money spent by my community will disappear with nothing to show for it. I fear the investors will lose what they contributed.

But most of all, I fear that Hina's voice will be lost forever.

I watch person after person cross before me – en route to something more important. Something more critical.

I set up my camp stove and I cook a few chickpeas, the way my wife would. They are rich with spice and the smell brings me to another place – a lush place far from the dry beginnings of a city on the Golan Heights.

It is then that I see her. A customer. A woman with a beautiful camera and two children in tow. One of the children has a huge gash on his head. *She* doesn't walk by. *She* stops. I step out from my tent to greet her.

She tries to speak to me in Arabic. And then in broken English. She doesn't ask to buy spices. She asks about my story. And then she photographs my tent and my bowls. She smells my chickpeas. I give her one. She tastes it, and she smiles. A deeply satisfied smile. No words are needed.

She asks what she should buy. She doesn't have a lot of money; the camera was from the life she had before. She just wants to try something. I recommend cardamom, and I tell her how to prepare it with rice. I sell her just enough for one meal. Just enough for her sons to appreciate the flavor.

She buys – the money is automatically transferred to my account, with the tax deducted – and she leaves.

Nobody else comes for the rest of the day. As the sun sets, I pack my spices back into their sealed containers. And then I cart them back out of the shuk and back to the flavorless campsite where I live.

I sold 15 Zuz in spice. My community invested about 25,000 Zuz in my endeavor, and I sold 15 Zuz, not counting expenses.

--

In the morning, I barely want to rise for prayers. My dream is a failure and I have destroyed others with it. I have nothing else to do, though. So, I get up from my mat, pray and then bring all of my belongings back to the shuk. On a whim, before I set up, I visit another stall and buy yogurt and almonds and tomatoes.

When I return to my place, I set out my spices and begin to prepare my breakfast. The same breakfast Hina made on that last day: May 28, 2010. Normally, I can't cook like her – but today everything seems to come out right. The chickpeas in the chole are spiced perfectly, the warm kulche bread feels lovely in my hands, and the kheer pudding is fragrant with nuts and cardamom. A sip of the yogurt chaas returns me to my shack – with her.

I am still sitting, dwelling inside that food, when the first customer arrives.

He is not from the City. He came from Israel. He read about my story and about my spices on the woman's blog. I share a morsel of my food and he buys a broad selection of my inventory.

Throughout the morning, more and more people come. Most are from the City. They too read about me. They too want to experience a bit of spice to add to their basic necessities.

I sell it to them too. A bit of this and a bit of that. Just enough for a meal or two.

Over the day, dozens of customers come. I sell 1,954 Zuz in spices.

I don't know what the next day will bring, but I know there is a future.

--

As I walk back to my campsite, something remarkable happens. I smell the flavors of the Punjab. All around me, my customers are cooking. They are cooking Hina's food.

The City, a world away from our paradise in the slums of Lahore, is filled with the echoes of her scent.

As I lay my head down to sleep, these are the scents that bathe my soul.

In the Torah portion of *KI-TAVO*, the nation is brought to life with eyes to see, ears to hear and a heart to know. It is brought to life and given a national soul.

There were many steps necessary to get to this place, steps that fill the last of Five Books. For me the most touching occurs in this reading. We are commanded to plaster stones with the words of Torah. It is a critical step in bringing the nation to life. But the Jewish people do not represent the first unified society in Torah. That distinction belongs to *BAVEL* (Babel).

If the text from the episode of *BAVEL* is read literally, it describes bricks being used in place of stone and the white being whitened and the dark being darkened. *BAVEL* replaced the natural with the uniformly manufactured and went through a process of eliminating the gray. The building blocks of that society had their humanity, and their human imperfections, removed. Theirs is a totalitarian model.

In this light, the plastering of the Torah shows us another way. The society described here is fashioned from stones – from the naturally imperfect. It is the words of Torah, which must be constantly renewed just as words on plaster are not permanent, that create our vision of perfection. This is a model that builds on our humanity, and relies on it. It is not one that eliminates our distinctions.

The attacks described in Lahore happened. Although no women were killed, the free-hand the attackers enjoyed was shocking even within Pakistan itself. The ideology that drove the attacks has much in common with *BAVEL*. It is an ideology that seeks to build a unified and perfect society by replacing human stones with inhuman bricks. The City serves as a contrast to this model. It brings together the unique and mismatched stones of many other societies, and uses them as the basis upon which a new plaster can be established.

Rather than eliminating the unique scents of Hina, the City integrates them in order to create something new and beautiful. I believe it can be a model for us all.

p.s. I originally wrote the Story of Hassan as I was fleshing out the ideas behind my book, the City on the Heights. Although many of the ideas behind this story are in the book, Hassan himself makes only a cameo appearance in one of the final chapters.

Nitzavim: The Minneapolis Lakes Savings & Trust

There are no walls in my new offices. Instead, each of my team's desks is shaped like a donut with a seat in the middle. They make me think of the battle stations on some sci-fi star cruiser; everybody's tools are close at hand, and there are no impediments to communication. All it takes to talk, *actually talk*, to anybody else in the room is the twist of a chair. The idea extends to the walls of the office itself. Instead of being located in some office park somewhere, the office takes up the entire 41st floor of a round building in downtown Minneapolis. With a glance around the room, my team members can connect with one another. With a glance out of the expansive windows, they can connect with the city they are serving.

Right now, the team is small. We have an entire floor of the building, but we don't use much of the space. The actual work area occupies only a small core of the center of the huge room. Today, my team members aren't alone, though. They've brought their families. I wouldn't have had it any other way. As I sit there, I watch, delighted, as young boys and girls race around the empty outer edges of the massive open room.

The children may not be using my office as an office, but they are using it well nonetheless.

I realize, with surprise, that even though my own family is not here, I am happier than I have ever been before.

And then, through the fog of my euphoria, I see one little boy at the far reaches of the room. He is just staring out the huge glass windows at the city below. I see him and I remember doing the exact same thing. In fact, my earliest memories are of standing in that exact same spot, watching that same city, and imagining what wonders my future would bring.

I had no idea what the world had in store for me. I've long since given up trying to guess.

I was born in 1966 to Benjamin Peterson and Sarah Peterson. I was born just one year after they were married. My father had been 62 years old then. He liked to claim that he'd taken so long to start a family because he'd been married to his business. But I knew the truth was more basic; it took him 62 years to find my mother.

For her part, my mother was 21 years younger than him. My father liked to joke that Sarah was his trophy wife. I could see another answer in their eyes, though. I knew that each of them could imagine no one more beautiful than the other.

All that aside, I wasn't raised by a man who could chase after me. Instead, he brought me to work. I literally grew up surrounded by my father's business, the Minneapolis Lakes Savings and Trust. The bank had survived the Great Depression in the stable hands of my grandfather. In those days, my family had given up their own home in an effort to avoid calling the loans of those they had lent their money to. It had almost all been for naught. In the end, the bank survived and the kindnesses my family had performed earned them the trust of the community. I grew up embraced by that community, and loved by it. Even a generation later, people in the Midwest remember the generosity of those around them.

My father had gotten his own start in the bank during the Great Depression. Eventually, he took over from his own father. And he grown the bank, albeit slowly. Eventually, he financed the very building I'm sitting in now. He financed the construction and then he bought one floor for the bank itself. The 41st floor. The one I'm sitting in right now. That's why I grew up looking out that window.

At first, it was in simple wonder. As time passed, though, my view began to change. The city was growing, but the bank seemed to stand still. My father was a child of the Great Depression and so he was a very conservative man. As I looked out the window, I began to see opportunities we had passed by. As I looked out the window, I began to see the obligations the city owed to my family.

I didn't only look out the window, of course. I also watched my father as he worked. At first, I admired everything he did. As I grew, though, I changed. I started to get bothered by my father's lenience with borrowers. He seemed too eager to forgive the obligations of others. All too often, or so I thought, my father used to hang up the phone after a difficult conversation and say, simply, 'there but for the grace of G-d go I.'

I didn't see things the way he did. Instead, I saw money that I was owed that would never be mine. All because people just did stupid things and weren't made to learn from them. They didn't buy insurance, they didn't put away savings, they spent more than they could afford, they ate too much and became sick. And then when their mistakes caught up to them, they begged my father to help them out. All too often, or so I thought, he did.

As I saw it, they didn't pay the price of their poor decisions. And if they didn't pay the price, they would never learn a better way.

I used to tell myself, as I watched my father patiently defer debt after debt, that the Great Depression was long over. My father's out-of-date ideas were stopping him from turning something good into something great.

I knew I could do better.

Like clockwork, I got my MBA, married a beautiful woman and bought a big house. When I was 25 years old, my reluctant father finally handed over the keys to the family business. What happened next became the stuff of business legend.

I thought at the time that I had simply been brilliant. I know now that I had simply been blessed with the miracle of timing.

I took over the bank just as the 1980s Savings and Loan Crisis was unfolding. Minneapolis Lakes Savings and Trust was a well-financed and unusually strong bank. I leveraged everything it had to buy distressed assets from all over the country. I revised my father's lenient policies and established a new – and extremely effective - debt-collection department. As I saw it, the more credit I could make available to people who could actually pay their debts, the better it would be both for me and for society as a whole.

By the end of the 1980s, I'd ditched the Minneapolis Lakes Savings and Trust name for the far simpler LakeCorp. The bank had become one of the largest in the United States. Unusually, it wasn't a public institution. Instead, I owned the whole thing. I bought the entire circular tower my father had once financed. I moved my own offices to the top floor, far above the 41st. When I looked out the window, I saw an empire. I could see that nothing had been left on the table. I'd taken a midsize regional bank and made it a colossus.

I was proud of what I'd done.

Eager for more, I surrounded himself with like-minded men. They were aggressive and powerful. They were doers. They had beautiful wives and homes. They inspired the jealousy of others. We were captains of industry. Even when we visited New York, the capital of finance, we were treated like royalty.

In 1989, at the age of 95, my father died. I showed up at his side at the last minute. We hadn't spoken in almost a decade and we barely spoke even then. The old man simply looked at me and said, quite simply, "Providence will show you the error of your ways."

I ignored the message.

Instead, I fulfilled my duty, waiting until the old man was gone. Then I went right back to work as if nothing had changed.

The bank kept growing and I bought more and more assets; from mortgages to mineral rights. Providence would teach me nothing. Diversification would protect me from the mistakes that had brought others down. That was just the way it worked.

I divorced my first wife in the mid-80s. She had been a trophy and she was a trophy no more. I married two more times. I didn't have much to do with my children. The way I saw it, they were simply there to keep my wives busy. I didn't resent the rich child support payments that followed my relationships. They were so generous that the press covered them. Like everything else, they were a sign of my incredible success.

Then, I got sick.

The sickness was nothing life-threatening. It was just a nasty bout of viral pneumonia. It was easily survivable for a 40-year-old man. But it took me out of the game. For just one week in September 2008, it took me out of the game.

It just so happened that that was the week Lehman Brother's collapsed. I knew then, and I know now, that I could have maneuvered through the resulting storm. People knew I paid my debts. They would have trusted me when I told them their patience would be rewarded. I *knew* I could have stabilized things long enough for calm waters to return.

But I was in a hospital bed – nearly delirious from the virus running through my body. When executives from Goldman Sachs or AIG or Bank of America called, I could not be reached. They, quite reasonably, thought I had lost my cool. They called their loans.

With asset prices severely depressed, the bank had to sell everything almost overnight. I went into the hospital a respected billionaire. I came out with my single largest asset wiped away from existence. Tens of thousands lost their jobs.

Of course, LakeCorp wasn't my only asset. It also wasn't my only obligation. Bit by bit, I found myself selling houses and cars. Before long I was living in a foul-smelling budget apartment in a complex I had once owned and I was driving an old beater of a Ford Explorer my gardener used to borrow. And, of course, my friends vanished. They weren't the kinds of people who associated with a failure. I couldn't blame them. I wasn't that kind of person either.

When I finally filed for bankruptcy, the national news followed the story. They soon lost interest though, and in the quiet months that followed, I took a job as a teller at a bank branch LakeCorp had once operated. But the storm had not yet passed. The bankruptcy had eliminated most of my obligations; but I had seven children from three different marriages and I owed child support for three of them. I had three minor children and no money to support them.

I pleaded with the courts to cut the payments, but they had little pity for a man who had been a billionaire the year before. They found me in contempt of court and with that, I lost my job as a bank teller. Broke, I moved into my car mere weeks before it broke down. Even after it died, I stayed in it. I had no place better to go. I hardly noticed when the courts cancelled my driver's license. They thought all my apparent poverty was simply a show. They were going to squeeze me into compliance.

I found a job stocking shelves in a nearby store. But I couldn't begin to make my payments. In 2015, I was arrested for contempt of court. I spent two horrifying weeks in jail. By the time I was released, my Ford Explorer had been towed and I had a criminal record. I wouldn't have hired me. Reluctantly, I moved into a downtown shelter and started panhandling at a freeway offramp.

I had nothing, not even a cellphone. As far as anybody could see, I was just another bum on the street. That was all I could see as well. My only reminder of my old life was that circular building. When I looked up from the freeway offramp, I could still see the window I used to stare out of as a child.

I guess it was natural that I began to hate myself. I was clean, I was able-bodied, I was well-educated and I was smart. I should have been able to meet at least some of my obligations. But I couldn't. Everything was beyond me.

One winter day when I was freezing in what passed for a coat, I realized that my father had been right. *Providence had showed me the error of my ways.*

I made myself a little sign then. It read "Jack Peterson, Banker." The second line read: "Must pay child support, please help." The way I thought of it, if I had nothing else to offer, at least I could serve as an example to others. The sign was kind of funny and so a local paper wrote it up. My story didn't suddenly change because of it. Instead, I spent day after day and month after month begging for child support at that freeway offramp.

My confidence was shattered and my hubris torn down.

As I looked at the drivers of the cars, I found myself saying what my father once had: "There but for the grace of G-d go I." I knew I deserved my fate.

One spring day, a man in a Honda Civic pulled up onto the shoulder next to me. He got out of his car and he asked, simply, "Are you really Jack Peterson?"

"Yes," I said, a bit confused.

"Are you the Jack Peterson who owns Grasslands Oil?"

I had to search my memory to know what he was talking about. Grasslands Oil had some worthless claims somewhere near the Rockies. It had been one of the assets so meaningless nobody had bothered to seize it.

"Yes," I answered, tentatively.

"We'd like to buy it," said the man.

The man offered only a few thousand dollars, but I wasn't an idiot. If they'd bothered to track me down at a freeway offramp; something more had to be at stake. I investigated and before long I realized what I had. A huge oil and gas find had occurred just a few miles from the claims I owned. That one abandoned asset was suddenly worth tens or even hundreds of millions of dollars.

Just like that, I was back in the game.

I was back in the game, but I wasn't the same man I'd been before. Debt and its repercussions had reinvented me. G-d had reinvented me. The very concept of interest gnawed at me. It was the most natural of things. Interest was charged because of the risk that another might not be able to repay. But I knew now that interest was not simply a passive acknowledgement of risk, it made that risk real. And along the way it created new and concrete consequences that supercharged the effects of unfortunate circumstance.

I knew, without debt, that I would never have suffered as I did.

And as I looked over the history of my family, I realized the dangers of debt were written throughout it all. A financial bust had almost destroyed my grandfather 80 years earlier. He had survived, earning the trust of his community along the way. But none of it had to happen. When the Great Depression came, and when the Great Recession came, asset values dropped and borrowers found themselves drowning in obligations they could not possibly fulfill. It was the chain of consequence, made real by debt, that raced upwards and claimed everybody it touched.

But Providence had taught me the error of my ways. And now, Providence had blessed me so I could find another road forward.

The first thing I did was buy back my father's old office. Then I moved into it, forgoing any sort of apartment. The place had a shower and that was all I needed. I moved into the office so I could spend all of my time planning. I had to find another road forward, but I didn't know what it was.

Bit by bit, as I stared out the office windows, my plans began to take form. A few months in, I began to hire my team. Instead of surrounding myself with hotshot bankers, I built a team of people who bought into my vision. I hired a lawyer excited to write up new kinds of contracts and an analyst stoked to develop new kinds of scoring and executives eager to raise the investment necessary to supercharge the idea and IT experts dedicated to developing the management systems that could make it all work. Finally, I hired salesmen eager to pitch my product to open-minded mortgage brokers. And I discovered something I hadn't expected. I discovered that I liked these people. I discovered that I loved them.

Now, I'm sitting at the conference table and a 32-year-old black woman named Susan Jones is sitting with me. Her husband and two children are at her side. In the world I'd once lived in, no circumstance would have brought us together. But it is circumstance that has brought her to me now. A health scare drove her into debt and her credit was destroyed. And then I met her. I visited her and I saw that she took excellent care of her possessions; the apartment she rents is clean and in good shape; her kid's toys all work. And she and her husband are conscientious about their jobs.

Susan Jones is not a rich woman, but her character shines through and I am proud to call her a friend.

And that is why she – a poor woman from a bad neighborhood – is about to sign an agreement with me, a man who was once the most powerful banker in America. The two of us are about to buy a house, together. She will own 20% and I will own 80%. She will pay rent on the 80%; to be set annually by a normally automated third-party assessor. Susan will have a fund to draw on for routine repairs while major repairs and renovations will have to be mutually agreed on. Critically, Susan will never be underwater. She'll own the same percentage of that house whether house prices rise or fall. If she stops paying rent then I will be able to sell her home, taking 80% of the proceeds. But she will still get her 20%.

As she is a part owner, I am confident Susan will take good care of the place. Both of us have a stake in the value of the home.

As a final incentive, Susan isn't stuck with 20% ownership. She will have the right to buy more of the house from me at any time, based on the most recent assessment of the property. Instead of a mortgage, and interest, we are invested, together, in an asset.

With that, so much danger is eliminated. Instead of realizing profit by giving life to risk, I will share in the ups and downs of my partners. I will create the reality my father and grandfather could only dream of; a reality in which a financial downturn does not destroy the families caught within it.

I look around the room once more. And I see the little boy is still standing there, looking out the window. I see him and I know what he sees. He sees what I saw when I was his age; a city filled with wonder.

But unlike me he won't grow up to see a city defined by lost opportunities, unmet obligations and fear. Instead, he will grow to see a city defined by hope and aspiration.

He will grow to see a city forever filled with possibility.

I smile again then, surrounded by the people I have come to love.

I pick up the pen in front of me. As if on cue, the crowd hushes and the children stop running.

Then, surrounded by sudden silence, I lean forward and sign the first of the Benjamin Patterson Mortgage Agreements.

The Torah reading of *NITZAVIM-VAYELECH* is described as a covenant with the nation. The covenant, also called a poem and a curse, is named as a witness against the Jewish people. As the reading puts it: "when many evils and troubles have befallen them, this poem shall testify against them as a witness."

These curses start with the people observing the idols of the nations that surround them. The idols are described as abominations (*SHEKETZ*), the only time idols are defined in such a way. But the idols are not only given a unique adjective, they are also given a unique noun. They are called *GELULAIM*. The word *GELUL* implies a cycle; it points to simple cause and effect in a world that goes around and around. The world of GELULAIM is a world without an historical arc and without a greater Divine plan. Unlike G-d, idols of wood and stone and silver and gold are inanimate servants of natural law. They are not truly alive. And their world, fully defined by cause and effect, is abominable to G-d.

The reading warns that, surrounded by this world, there will be those who claim *"I shall have peace though I walk in the stubbornness of my heart."* They deny there is a greater morality at work. As the nation is rotted by those described as headstrong and intentional sinners, the nation will come to be cursed. It will become an example to all the nations.

Only when the people recall the curses recorded in this reading will they be ready to return to G-d. Only then will they be brought back to their land and be showered by G-d's blessings. They will be redeemed, but they will not be the same people they had been before. Their desire to ignore G-d will have been erased and they will embrace Hashem with all their hearts and all their souls.

In this story, Jack Peterson goes through the same process as the people of Israel. He worships a world of cause and effect. He sees a world without intent. He is headstrong and stubborn. In his story, his father's admonitions serve as a warning for him. They serve as the song-witness described in this story. When everything conspires against him it is this witness – the last words of his father – that opens the door to his redemption.

It is only when he is begging on the side of the freeway offramp that he understands the source of his suffering and is ready to be freed of it.

It is only then that he can dedicate himself to Providence.

Shabbat Shalom.

p.s. I chose a banker for this story for a few reasons. First, S'DOM and AMORA are mentioned as prior examples of the curses the people will face. While S'DOM and AMORA had no problem paying their obligations (offering payment to Avraham for his rescue), they are places that offered nothing to those who had not earned it, even travelers. Perhaps they feared the impact of such decisions. S'DOM and AMORA were places of creation without holiness; charity was beyond them.

Second, later in the reading, the SHMITA year, the year in which debts are forgiven, is also mentioned. It is during the SHMITA year that the Torah is read as a reminder of the values of Hashem. The SHMITA represents yet another of the Torah's attacks on the reality of interest and debt. These attacks run throughout the Chumash. Debt focuses on the risks in our world; that is how it is priced. It gives life to risk and reality to evil. Even if all goes well, debt finance enables people to dedicate years of future earnings to the acquisition of assets. This, all by itself, drives the price of those assets up far beyond what would otherwise be affordable.

In contrast to debt, equity investments like the Benjamin Peterson Mortgage Fund are built on opportunity and give reality to the good.

Vayeilech: The Barn

As I walk towards the barn, the smell of the hay is amazing to me. There are so many things I can no longer smell. They've just vanished, bit by bit from my reality. All of my senses have been dulled. It is almost as if I've been retreating from this world.

The path to the barn has no paving. Once, there were two parallel dirt tracks, overgrown with weeds. They were made by the tractors and horse-drawn trailers that used to make their way to the barn. But decades have passed since then. Today, there is only one thin track, a string of dirt meandering gently to capture the smoothest sections of what once was a makeshift road.

I have to concentrate when I walk now, it is no longer so easy to walk. Even with my cane prodding the ground, ensuring that my feet meet solid ground, I know I can still fall at any moment.

Everything has been dulled. I know there are birds, but I cannot hear them. Even if I could, I would not listen. To me, right now, the world consists only of myself and the track I am following.

I am retreating and I know that *this* may well be the last time I follow it.

I used to walk this path when I was a child. I would run it, as often as not, leaving the smell of my mother's fried eggs behind as I ran towards my father's barn. My memory of that smell is stronger than any 'real' smell has been in years.

A long time has passed since I was a boy.

At last, I come to the end of the track. The barn door is old and rusted. The barn itself is almost stereotypical. It is a deep red and several stories tall with a gentle rounded shape. It would have been a proud building once. But not anymore. The paint has been darkened by weather. Old windows have been boarded over. It looks derelict and empty. But I know that it isn't.

I grasp the metal handle of the door and then I pull. I pull with everything I have. My arms ache with the effort. I can't put much force into the effort. Nonetheless, slowly, with the screech of rusted metal, the door slides open.

It is dark inside, but it doesn't take long for my eyes to adjust. I know what to expect.

There is no hay inside. Instead, the space inside is filled by shapes. Shapes covered with tarps.

My father worked in the barn, but he was no farmer. He'd kicked out the horses and loaded the place up with his equipment. He was a sculptor. When he started a new piece, he'd begin with tiny, simple, models. Slowly, he'd make more and more intricate forms. Then the scale would increase until he had a singular giant wax model. Of course, wax was not the ultimate material. In a careful process, he would create huge plaster forms around the wax and then pour paraffin into those forms. Then, he would delicately shape clay all around the core paraffin model and even within it. Finally, he would pour molten copper into the void between the clay layers. The paraffin would melt away and a bronze statue would be left behind.

It was incredible delicate work. Delicate and expensive.

The casting itself was an art, to say nothing of the pieces he sculpted.

My father used to tell me, lovingly, that he did his work the same way the ancient Greeks had done it. In a way, he said, his work was timeless.

Few people worked that way anymore, at least on that scale. Modern welding techniques and modern materials had made the process simpler. But my father didn't seek simplicity. His sculptures had an ancient feel to them, a feeling he cultivated. At the same time, his subject matter was thoroughly modern. His most famous piece was of a man sitting in the back of a cab, his eyes pensively watching as an unseen city passes by his window. All the statue had was the corner of his bench seat, a touch of the door and the man himself. And yet everything was evoked. Everyone who saw it was pulled into the reality my father had created.

He was considered a modern master.

When I was a little boy, I used to wonder at the work of his hands. To me, he was the greatest of men and could do no wrong. His barn was a treasure house of all that was perfect in the world.

I didn't stay a boy. I grew up. And I began to understand more of what he did. I began to understand the expense. I also began to understand the profits. My father made millions. And slowly, his art – in my mind at least – was replaced by the money it made.

I began to think that that was why he did what he did.

When I was in high school, he would drone and on about his technique. He would spend dinner talking, ad nauseam, about how a sculpture – a great sculpture – can reach across time.

Bit by bit, I learned to tune him out. Everything he said just turned to meaningless noise. As I saw it, he was pretentious and he was preachy.

I asked him once, about the money. He brushed me aside, saying the money wasn't why he did what he did.

"So, why?" I asked him, "Do you charge so much?"

He smiled then and said that, for some people, money was among the most important things. They invested in his pieces, and made them a part of themselves, precisely because they spent huge sums on them.

It seemed like a self-serving argument. Like he too was acknowledging the importance of the money. But he didn't spend his money. We lived in a small house in a small town. Maybe he felt guilty about what he had? The idea disgusted me.

I started to see my father as a hypocrite. I stopped going to the barn.

I couldn't understand what my father was doing. With all this money, why didn't he go and see the world? Why not travel? Why not enjoy the finer luxuries in life? Why were we driving old cars and living in the middle of nowhere, surrounded by country hicks?

Things only got worse from there. He started delivering angry speeches around the dinner table, condemning my short-sightedness. I totally tuned him out.

One time, he told me that if I did not change my ways, I would grow old and die alone – with nothing to pass on or share. I just ignored him. Like the smell of fried eggs, he just began to recede from my reality.

After all, life was too short to spend it worrying about old age.

My mother died when I was 16. Maybe he thought it would change me. I certainly thought it would change him. How could he not travel, now? But nothing changed. Tensions just grew in the house. It turned out she'd been the only one holding us together. I moved out when I was 18, as soon as I could. I went to college at a state school *far* from our little homestead. And I had nothing more to do with the old man.

He died when I was 23. At least he left me his money.

His will ended with a simple sentence: "I know you will return."

I knew I wouldn't.

Unlike my father, I spent his money well. I enjoyed the finer things. I had beautiful girlfriends and cars and houses. I travelled. I enjoyed life thoroughly, exploring and learning and *living*.

Sometimes I would think of him and his foolishness.

But I knew I had done 'Life' better.

I was thirty-eight years old when the cash finally began to run out. I sold a few things. Some cars. A few houses. I started travelling less. And then I remembered the old homestead. *That* I could sell and not miss in the least.

For the first time in decades, I travelled home.

I drove up the old driveway. The house was in terrible shape. It had been abandoned for twenty years and it showed. It wouldn't be worth much. I made my way back to the barn. Perhaps some of the equipment would be salvageable. But the barn was locked. I tried to jimmy the lock, but I couldn't manage it. I called for a locksmith and together we managed to pull open the door to the old building.

As the first light was cast into the vast space, I didn't understand what I was seeing.

Inside there were shapes, everywhere. They were covered by tarps. I walked into the barn, flashlight in hand. I walked towards the first of the shapes. With a tug, I pulled the tarp back and I revealed a sculpture I'd never seen before. It was a sculpture of a man and a boy.

It was a sculpture of my father and me.

The boy was pointing, excitedly, at something.

And the man is watching the boy, smiling deeply at the scene.

It was a sculpture of my childhood.

In that moment, that image ripped at my heart. That sculpture condemned me. I'd lived a life of luxury, but I didn't have *this*. His work would survive, but nothing of mine would.

His sculptures condemned me as his words never had.

I began to walk through the barn, that day, uncovering more and more of the shapes. I didn't understand them all, not then. But somehow, they seemed to understand *me*. I felt like a child again, awe-struck by his work. These sculptures were the best my father had ever done, and nobody had ever seen them.

For a moment, I thought of how much they would be worth. I could live the rest of my life off of these works. But I knew, even as I thought it, that I could not sell them. They were never meant to be sold.

I moved into that decrepit house, almost penniless. I took a job at the local grocery and I began fixing up the house. Every day, I made my way down to the barn. Every day I drank in what my father had left behind.

And every day I pictured what he had warned me of; that I would end up here old and broken and alone. Then his work would pass to others and his message to me would be for naught.

I have come back every day since, my heart finally open to what my father had been saying. But there is still so much I do not understand.

Today is no different. Except, of course, I am a much older man. I am old. And I am physically broken.

I am old. But I am not alone.

A little girl dashes past me and into the barn. Her blond hair flies out behind her.

"Grace, slow down, Grace!" I hear her mother call. And I smile. A screaming batch of other kids stream after Grace.

A year after I moved back to my hometown, I met a young widow who had moved to the town from New York. We married, and had two children.

And, now, we have eight grandkids. Including Grace.

Every year, the whole family comes back here, to my own father's gallery. We drink in what he left for us.

As she enters the barn, Grace skids to a halt. And then she looks up at one of the sculptures. Her excited expression suddenly changes to one of awe.

I know the feeling; I had it when I was her age.

"Grandpa," she says, looking at me. "What is this one?"

I follow her gaze. I look at the sculpture.

I've seen it a million times, but only *now* do I know what it is.

It is a sculpture of me, an old and stooped man.

And flying by me, pigtails hanging in the wind, is a little girl.

Flying by me, is Grace.

This story closely mirrors the Torah reading of VAYEILECH. In this reading, Moshe is passing the baton on to future generations; but even as he does, he knows the coming generations will go astray. They will abandon the timeless values of Hashem. So, Moshe pushes his successor to be strong and of good courage. But his work does not stop there. He tells them to come, young and old, to hear the HAKEL – the recitation of Torah. It is meant to be a reminder, like the annual visit to the barn, of the values that matter.

Moshe doesn't leave it there though. He leaves a copy of the Torah itself next to the timeless ark. He leaves it as a timeless witness, like Heaven and Earth, to condemn the mistakes of his people. Ultimately, I believe, he leaves it as a reminder to us of why we exist and what is important.

Today, we still have that witness. It is waiting for us, left behind by our ancestors and meant to be shared with those yet to come.

Today, like the man in the story (or perhaps the little girl), we still come back to *our* barn. We still revisit the timeless. And we still see ourselves there. And we are rejuvenated by the vision of what has been and what is yet to be.

This story was written in honor of a co-worker's father, Charles Phillip Swain, who died Thursday.

As my co-worker wrote to me:

My Dad was a great human, fallible, forgiving yet yearning for better of everyone. His dad died when he was in early twenties. I am certain he loved being dad to his son(s) and giving back in grown children what he didn't have a chance to get.

His life was a life fulfilled, no matter the surprises along the journey.

May we know only joy.

Ha'azinu: The Banishment of Eve

Ruth Marquet sat in front of her bank of computer monitors, crying. On her screens, fed to her through a live satellite and drone feed, were the images of a teenage girl. She was 16 and she was being attacked on the street by a growing mob of people.

Her name was Eve and she was Ruth's daughter.

Eve was crying for help. Calling out to the sky for her mother's rescue. But Ruth was not helping. She was just watching, crying, as a mob engulfed her only child.

Ruth Marquet had never intended to have a child. She wasn't the type. Ruth Marquet was a killer. She didn't work for some government or even as a criminal gun for hire. She did it on her own; as her unique gift to the world. As far as most anybody else knew, she was an AI specialist. She ran a company that designed artificial intelligence systems meant to cut through all the noise of modern life. This stuff would tell you what was really important, when it was really important. It was useful. She knew this because hundreds of millions of people used it. But it was just a byproduct of her real interest.

When nobody was looking, she killed bad guys. She knew she was police, prosecutor and judge. She was okay with that. She investigated her targets thoroughly and struck only those who were, due to corruption or a broken civil society, beyond the reach of effective law enforcement. She was like a superhero. She probably seemed that way to her targets. Her specialty wasn't long-range sniping attacks or stealthy one-man operations. Her power came from the software she had designed; in fact, it was why she had designed it. Her AI system helped her coordinate a virtual army of technological devices simultaneously. When she attacked a target, she would deploy a suite of monitoring and attack systems to support and reinforce her efforts. She combined numerous drone feeds and signaling systems into her augmented reality vision and audio system. She had remotely operated explosives, proximity sensors and autonomous defensive units to watch her back. She thought sometimes that she was like a many-handed goddess of death, surrounded by her angels.

Despite all her technology, she never used her robots to kill her targets. Certainly, their security teams might die this way, but never the targets themselves. Instead, she would emerge from the center of her web of electro-magnetic terror and finish the job herself. She felt she *had* to do this. There was something disrespectful about taking her target's lives by remote control.

She had to do it herself.

All of this, she knew, made her entirely unsuitable as a mother.

Ruth was an incredibly accomplished and wealthy woman. She lived in an actual fortress (it came with the trade). She knew she had done a lot of good in the world.

Then, one day, there was nobody left to kill.

It wasn't that humankind disappeared or suddenly became righteous. It was something else entirely. Something that had snuck up on Ruth. She had been so busy with her work that she hadn't noticed the phenomenon that had overrun the world.

It was called Connect.

Connect was a pill, although Ruth had no idea what it was made of. When you took it, you entered another world. Not an alternate reality or a world of hallucinations, you entered a world of telepathic communication. You could communicate, purely and directly, with others taking the drug. It was incredibly addictive. Connect spread like wildfire and people took it and disappeared from the 'real' world, hooked. It was like a zombie movie. They lost weight because they neglected to eat. They were disheveled and disgusting.

There were debates among the few holdouts in the real world. There were debates about whether this drug was a good idea. On the positive side, people had been blessed with incredibly close relationships. They had also made their own choice to take the drug. Also, the effects of the drug didn't seem to diminish with use. Users didn't sink into unhappiness. But Ruth did not see this. She saw people living in the moment, with raw emotions sweeping the entire planet almost instantaneously. Within months, the vast majority of human society was hooked. That included those Ruth Marquet would typically have targeted. They were no longer criminal masterminds. They let themselves become simple Connectors.

Ruth, though, was a hold out. There were others who resisted the drug, who saw something worthwhile in the 'real' world. But they were few and far between, and they didn't tend to survive for long. Mobs of half-present Connectors would descend on them, taking their possessions and sharing the pleasure of their hunt with the world.

Ruth could hold out. She had means few other people had. She had a garden patch within the high walls of her home. Something to keep her sane. And she had access to a world of data, something to keep her safe. The problem was, by the time she worked out where Connect had come from, it was too late to act. It wasn't that there hadn't been an inventor. It was that the drug was being manufactured by the users themselves. There was no evil mastermind to strike.

Perhaps there had been, but he had long since disappeared into the mass of humanity.

Ruth watched this. Her own power systems supplied electricity to her network of drones. Her AI systems hacked into unguarded satellite signals. She watched from her control room as emotional spasms ripped through the planet, and humankind moved like a teeming mass of insects. They ate what they found, quickly losing huge numbers to starvation, but they kept teeming – one great mind, mindlessly consuming the world around it.

Ruth didn't know what to do. She couldn't kill all of mankind. Well, she could have. She could have stolen smallpox and various weaponized viruses and she could have personally removed the survivors. It wouldn't have accomplished anything, though. She needed to raise mankind up, not destroy it.

She needed humankind to know what it was missing.

It was then, meditating on this challenge, that she realized she needed a child.

It wasn't terribly difficult to accomplish the necessary pre-cursor steps. A few hospitals had independent power sources designed for very long-term outages. They were outposts in a desert of destruction. A few of those facilities had fertility clinics stocked with the genetic material of an appropriate range of potential fathers. Susan screened these as best as she could, poring through hospital records and even carrying out a little analysis of her own. And then she chose the biological father and took the first steps to becoming a mother.

He found him in a desert land, and in the waste, a howling wilderness.

Childbirth was risky. She studied intensively, trying to develop the skills necessary to intercede in an emergency. She developed a robot to manage the delivery and other systems to intercede in case things went wrong. She secured blood supplies from a nearby hospital. She set up autonomous security for her labor. She did everything she could, because humankind depended on it.

Then, almost without incident, she gave birth to Eve.

In that moment, Rush discovered she was a mother after all.

As her baby looked at her through unfocused newborn eyes, Ruth realized that Eve was the most beautiful thing she had ever seen. Ruth discovered that she would do anything for her.

For the portion of the LORD is His people, Jacob the lot of His inheritance. He compassed him about, He cared for him, He kept him as the apple of His eye.

Eve was a blessing Ruth had never known she needed. Nonetheless, she remained a tool. She existed to save mankind. So, Ruth did not just want her daughter's happiness, Connect might have supplied that. No, she wanted her daughter's fulfillment.

Eve was well fed, secure and accomplished. Ruth would work her little garden and Eve would help; even as a toddler she could carry seeds for her mother. Eve lived well, with gifts and luxuries the world had long since otherwise lost.

He made him ride on the high places of the earth, and he did eat the fruitage of the field; and He made him to suck honey out of the crag, and oil out of the flinty rock;

The idea was simple: the Connectors would see Eve, they would want to be like Eve, and the drug that held them would begin to lose its grasp. Then, one by one, Ruth could pull people out, blessing them with her powers and helping them join her in farming and building and engaging with objectives greater than those Connect could offer.

Through blessings and relationships, Ruth could counter the nihilism of Connect.

It didn't work out that way. As she grew older, Eve became aware that she was not there simply to live. She realized she was being used for another purpose. It dug at her. And then one day, she found and took Connect. She entered the world her mother had forbidden to her.

Of the blood of the grape thou drankest foaming wine. But Jeshurun waxed fat, and kicked...

Ruth, of course, had seen it happen. But what could she do? If she forced her daughter not to take the pill, her resistance would grow. She would desire it more. The rest of humankind would learn that Ruth's path was one of coercion, not fulfillment. She could support her daughter, despite the drug. But then the world would learn that Ruth's blessings followed her child. They would not understand that Ruth's gifts were reserved for those who followed a better path.

There was something else, something less analytical that drove Ruth's decision just to watch. Ruth was angry. Her daughter had rejected all that she had done for her. She had followed the foreign allure of Connect.

O foolish people and unwise? is not He thy father that hath gotten thee? hath He not made thee, and established thee?... They roused Him to jealousy with strange gods, with abominations did they provoke Him.

And so, angry and jealous and having no other options, Ruth drove her daughter, humankind's only daughter, from her little compound. She watched as the rest of the world convulsed with her decision, the emotions almost instantly travelling from her corner of the planet to humanity as a whole. Ruth knew what the world would do. They would hate Eve. Eve was a repudiation to the most fundamental decision they had ever taken in their lives. Eve's very existence cried out against the use of Connect. Eve might think she was joining humankind, fitting in with a world gone mad. But the world would know that Eve saw herself as a path to redemption – it was how she had been raised and she could not hide it. Not with Connect. No, the world would never accept her. Instead, they would make an example of her.

The first attack came only a few hours after Eve left. There were a few of them. Ruth could not sense their conversation, but she could guess at it. The others would hate Eve. Eve would try to assure them that she was one of them. But their hate would only grow. Eve would never belong. It was inevitable. Then, as Ruth watched, they attacked. They would make an example of Eve Marquet.

But they were no match for Eve – well-fed Eve. They lost quickly, but they hurt Eve in the process.

Ruth just watched.

But Eve, foolish Eve, kept going. She desperately wanted to join the world.

They sacrificed unto demons, no-gods, gods that they knew not, new gods that came up of late

And Ruth just watched.

And the LORD saw, and spurned, because of the provoking of His sons and His daughters.

Ruth watched as the mobs came. Her daughter was beaten and scratched and bruised and attacked. And, with her satellites and drones, Ruth just watched. She just watched as her daughter cried out for help. She cried with the pain of it, but Ruth ignored her. The child needed to learn. The world needed to learn. They needed to learn the darkness of Connect. They needed to learn the darkness of abandoning Ruth's path.

And He said: 'I will hide My face from them, I will see what their end shall be; for they are a very forward generation, children in whom is no faithfulness.

Ruth just watched. Her daughter survived. She was strong. But she suffered terribly. She knew how to plant, not forage. And insect-like humanity had stripped the land clear. She could not compete with them. She grew hungry and thirsty and tired.

The wasting of hunger, and the devouring of the fiery bolt, and bitter destruction; and the teeth of beasts will I send upon them, with the venom of crawling things of the dust.

And Ruth watched.

Her anger only grew as her daughter pushed further away. She demanded help, but made no move to return. And for a cold moment, Ruth thought she would abandon her completely and allow her to be destroyed.

I thought I would make an end of them; I would make their memory cease from among men;

But then she realized she could not do this. Nothing would be achieved.

Were it not that I dreaded the enemy's provocation, lest their adversaries should misdeem, lest they should say: Our hand is exalted, and not the LORD hath wrought all this.'

She wished her daughter had understood. She wished she had embraced her mother's path. But she had not. She was only a foolish child.

For they are a nation void of counsel, and there is no understanding in them.

133

Ruth saw when Eve turned back, back towards home. She saw when Eve changed her path. She saw when her daughter finally began to understand. It was then that Ruth left her fortress. Like a goddess of death, she came among her daughter's tormentors. And in anger, she struck them down.

If I whet My glittering sword, and My hand take hold on judgment; I will render vengeance to Mine adversaries, and will recompense them that hate Me. I will make Mine arrows drunk with blood, and My sword shall devour flesh; with the blood of the slain

She realized that this too was an example. Her daughter's example would be one of life. Those who could not accept her, those who defended Connect, would suffer. Ruth would offer both joy and pain. And so, Ruth fought, leaving an example of vengeance that spread the world over.

Sing aloud, O ye nations, of His people; for He doth avenge the blood of His servants, and doth render vengeance to His adversaries, and doth make expiation for the land of His people.

She fought and then she brought Eve home. She nursed her back to health. She could yet be an example to the world. She could still raise up humanity. It was, after all, why she had been created.

He said unto them: 'Set your heart unto all the words wherewith I testify against you this day; that ye may charge your children therewith to observe to do all the words of this Torah. For it is no vain thing for you; because it is your life, and through this thing ye shall prolong your days upon the land, whither ye go over the Jordan to possess it.'

Her girl had left as a child, but she had returned a woman. Ruth saw her and smiled. And she realized once again that Eve was the most beautiful thing she had ever seen.

She discovered that she would do anything for her.

I've always found the reading of *HA'AZINU* very hard to embrace. G-d seems like the worst kind of jealous husband. We cheat and he allows us to be hurt and damaged and assaulted. Then He returns to us, destroying those we had left Him for so that we are protected from our own sin. All of this is somehow justified because we were created to fulfill the Torah. I've struggled with this image; I wrote this story to grapple with it.

Now I think I can understand it. We exist to bless the world and raise it up. We are G-d's tool in this effort. Despite this, we often abandon G-d. And He, in turn, hides His face from us. The cycle in this reading: of blessing, abandonment, suffering and return is meant to teach us, and ultimately the world, the path of G-d. It is meant to free us from the values that flow through our world, pulling us away from true fulfillment.

In an era when so many raise children to be happy, this reading holds out another paradigm. Perhaps we should seek something greater than our children's joy. Perhaps we should raise them to create, invest in the holy and relate to our Creator, the Holy One, Blessed be He.

V'Zot Haberacha: The Institution

The weather is wonderful today. The heat of the summer has passed and the autumn air seems to caress us. I can *smell* the stones on the buildings that surround me. They smell old and worn and wise. I love their smell in the autumn. But what truly grabs me tonight is not the weather, but the sounds. I am in a Sukkah, but it is not like other Sukkot. Mine is a Sukkah in a special place. An institution.

A place I am not allowed to leave.

It is a place I haven't left in fifteen years.

We're normally allowed out in the courtyard. That isn't unusual. But the courtyard is surrounded by high fences and dilapidated old buildings of Jerusalem stone. We can hear street noises filtering over the walls and buildings that surround us. We can have some distant sense of Jerusalem, the city the institution is part of. But those street noises just dig at our souls, reminding us of where we cannot be. They remind us of what we do not have. The courtyard normally finds a way to feel more like a prison than the cells themselves.

Somehow, though, Sukkot is different. We can hear families having meals in their own Sukkot. The sounds of the holiday come at us from every direction. As I hear them today, a verse flows through my mind: "Matovu Ohalecha Yaacov" – "How Goodly are your Tents oh Jacob."

I smile, a rare thing these days. I smile and I listen. We all do. All of us patients, crowded into our Sukkah, just listen. All the other Sukkot are sources of life and sound and conversation. But we are silent, just drinking in the joy of our people.

Only months ago, I was diagnosed with an aggressive melanoma; far too late to do anything about it. I probably have months to live. I know I will live for that time in *this* place. This Institution. I'll never experience the streets of Jerusalem again. I'll never experience family again. All I'll ever have is the sounds of this Sukkot holiday. All I can do is transport myself in my mind, imagining myself among the families that surround me. I can smell their meals. I can hear their conversations. I can feel their love. In some little way, I can relive what I've lost.

I first heard the voice of G-d when I was six years old. At least that's what I thought I heard. It is funny, to have such an experience and not be sure. I was in cheder, learning to read the Shema. The Rebbe paused and I looked around, kind of bored. And then there was a voice, out of nowhere. It wasn't the Rebbe's voice. It wasn't the voice of any of the other children. It was deep and clear. It spoke only a few words, but somehow, I couldn't make out what they were. Perhaps I was so shocked by it that I didn't hear it clearly. I asked the Rebbe if he had spoken, but he said no. But he joked that perhaps I had been hearing the voice of G-d. 'Shema Yisrael', 'Hear oh Israel.' My name was – is – Yisrael. It was kind of clever, but he shouldn't have said it. I was so flustered by the whole thing that I couldn't recall, even then, what was said. Was it a prophecy, a message, a mission? I had no idea.

All I had known was that I had heard *something*.

I didn't hear that voice again, not for years. I still wasn't a normal child, though. I was distracted by all the wrong things. I was overwhelmed by sights and sounds and people. It was like I didn't know how to filter between signal and noise. All the things others learned how to dismiss – the sounds of traffic, pieces of trash on the street, the buzz of lightbulbs – I *couldn't* dismiss. I couldn't filter what was important and what was irrelevant. I hadn't even been in a normal cheder when I was six years old. I had been in a special cheder for children with special needs.

The voice came back, the same voice, when I was twelve years old. I was ready for it then. I listened to it. I realized then why I hadn't understood it in cheder. It didn't deliver instructions to me. Or even a sentence. It just stated the names of the Jewish tribes. Reuven, Levi, Yehuda, Issacher and so on. I would look at people and the voice would say a name: Reuven. Every time I looked at the person, the same name would be stated. I couldn't shut it out. It encircled me, adding to the stimulations I couldn't control. It became more and more frequent until it became a constant in my life. I remember breaking down, my arms flailing in an incredible fit. I was in a mall; the names were being shouted at me. I just couldn't take it. I closed my eyes and screamed. My mother was embarrassed, deeply embarrassed. She asked me to stop. She begged me to stop. But I couldn't. She carried me out of there, brought me home, and locked me in my room. I settled then. The voice disappeared. There were no people to see. I *knew* all the sounds of my room. I could put them in their places. I could regain my control.

I'd read once about animals that would flee ahead of a fire or hunker down in anticipation of an earthquake. I read that some scientists thought they could sense the fire or the vibrations of the quake. I thought maybe people could too, but we'd learned to filter those things out. We learned to ignore those signals. Perhaps I was like the animals. Perhaps I hadn't learned to filter out what everyone could hear. Perhaps I was the only one living in reality.

It made sense. But for the voice. It was so urgent, so loud, so repetitive. It was insistent. "GAD!" "MENASHE!" ... I couldn't imagine not hearing it, no matter how tuned out I became.

My family wasn't an exception when it came to the voices. I would see my father or my brothers or my mother and the word "YOSEF!" would be shouted at me. I couldn't bear even to have Shabbat dinner in my own home. The voice struck at me, relentless in its call. My parents pulled me from school and they brought me to a doctor. She (EPHRAIM!) prescribed powerful anti-hallucinogens. They made my whole world dull and dark, like I had a dim and quiet smartphone and I couldn't turn up the brightness or volume.

The drugs had no effect on the voice, though. They had no effect on what my family was trying to combat.

One day, I was in my room and a thought occurred to me. Perhaps the voice wanted me to record what it was saying. Perhaps that was where the urgency came from. So, I wrote my father's name in a book. And next to it, I wrote "Yosef."

And then, fearful, I walked from my room and I approached my father. He was sitting on a chair in our living room, reading from a sefer. I looked at him, nervous. He looked at me, concerned and confused and full of love. There was no voice! I almost cried with relief. I ran back to my room and I began to write, furiously. Every person I could think of was attached to a name. I filled out page after page, scrawling maniacally. Then I left my home.

I wandered into the dim world and I saw my neighbors. But the voice did not scream at me. I had recorded what it had said, and it was satisfied. When I wandered further from my home, the voice came back. I would write down the names of the tribes, but nothing would happen. The voices would not go away, I needed to know *who*

I was seeing. I had to write down *their* names. And so, I began to research people. With the voice in my head hammering away I would ask people *who* they were. I was only a child. I pretended it was part of a school project. I would write down their names, and next to them the name of their tribe. And the voice would be silenced. I began to carry a notebook everywhere I went. But I tried not to go too many places. Home was safe. School was safe. The streets between got safer and safer with every passing day. The whole neighborhood knew about my school project. They didn't understand it of course, but they were kind enough. They would give me their names and I would write them down in my little notebook. And the voice would go away.

One day, there was no voice. I had recorded everybody I saw. I felt safe then, secure. I thought of the next day being the same. But when I awoke, the voice was saying something else "Evarech" – "I will bless." It was like a mantra, occasional and quiet at first. But it got louder and louder. And, somehow, I knew what it wanted. I *had* to leave my house. I had to *seek out* Jews I did not know. And I had to write down their names and record the tribe they belonged to.

So, I did. I left my home. I sought out others. People were suspicious of me. Was I some kind of fraudster? Was I trying to pry their personal data for some nefarious purpose? I never asked for addresses, but they were suspicious, nonetheless. They didn't understand what I was doing.

I didn't understand what I was doing.

But I did it nonetheless. It was the only way I could live.

In time, I *could* live with the voices. I travelled every day – around Jerusalem and around Israel. I sought out Jews, but I was surprised by others – living in the land – who had a tribe connected to then. I recorded names and tribes. Slowly my life became more normal. I was slapped with the occasional complaint: fearful people (particularly women) justifiably uneasy about my intrusions. But I cut back on my medications and for the most part, I became more normal.

I met a woman one day and I asked her her name and she asked me why. And I showed her the book. I somehow thought that it was right to show it to *her*. I explained what I thought I was doing. And she asked me what tribe she belonged to. She was serious and curious and engaged. And I told her: Zevulun. Her face lit up. She found it *beautiful*. Not beautiful in a pitying way, or a cute one. Just *beautiful*. She recited the blessing in the final Torah reading of V'Zot Haberacha. She recited it by heart: "Rejoice Zevulun in your going out." I asked her why she knew it. She'd been studying it that morning. She'd wondered what it meant. So, she'd gone out, just to understand. She told me her name, Miriam. I wrote it down.

We married not long after. She overlooked – ignored – my many problems. Under the Chupah she changed to a Yosef. I brought a notebook for the occasion, surreptitiously collecting her new identity as it shifted. Silencing the voice so I could continue with the celebration.

We lived a pretty normal life. I didn't learn in Kolel or get a job. But she knew I couldn't. I travelled, constantly, collecting names and tribes in my tiny volumes.

We had a child. A baby girl. Chaya, also of Yosef. She was born after Yom Kippur. I wrote down her name and we celebrated Sukkot then; thankful for the gifts of G-d, embracing the troubled reality we'd been given. The joy was palpable that first year. And the second as well.

And then one day, two years later, there was a murder. I had been nearby – without any other understandable kind of business – when it happened. I was the weird man who asked for peoples' names. I was the freak who wouldn't give up until people told me. I was the one who walked funny, or broke down at the strangest times, who fled from people but thrust himself among them. I was identified as the sick man who had taken a woman's life.

I hadn't taken her life. I had just happened to have been there moments after it had happened. The police found my notebooks – they filled our home. The courts decided I was not fit to stand trial. And I was condemned, locked up in a mental institution. My 'normal' life was over.

Now I am dying here. I am listening to the voices from the Sukkot all around me. And I'm dying. And what for? What have I achieved? Why have I suffered? My wife loves me, but I see her so infrequently. My daughter hates me, and it is made worse because I see her so infrequently. She's seventeen now. She's not religious, not like my wife and I. Her father's a delusional killer, her mother loves him. And my daughter? She'd runs from anything to do with either one of us. Perhaps she fears becoming what we have become.

But I'm dying. And so, this Sukkot, she has agreed to see me one more time. I look up as one of the orderlies opens a door on the side of one of the old buildings. I watch my wife, my beautiful Miriam walk into the Sukkah. With her is my daughter Chaya, angry, sullen, and resentful.

We sit then. And we have a meal together. Like we had in days of old. We remember the Sukkot – Miriam and I – that we had once celebrated. I remember that joy. I live it one last time. And I wonder again – I ask G-d again – "why have I been sentenced to such pain and such suffering?" I ask, within my own heart, what has been accomplished? My notes, my copious notes, would vanish.

All would be lost.

And would it even be a tragedy? Is any of it even real? Or is it just the collected delusions of a sick child and a dangerous man?

I look at my daughter. She is still sullen and angry. Her eyes are downcast. And I remember the blessing of Yosef: *Mimeged.* It is a word that appears no place else in the Five Books of Moses. Mimeged. The indirect blessing. The heaven to dew, the sun to grain, the moon to children, great heights to mystery, land and fullness.

The beautiful, indirect, blessing. And I wonder how I could bless my daughter, this last time. I wonder what I could leave her with.

What will be best for a daughter of Yosef?

I feel the words come to me. She looks away from me as I lay my hands on her head and I say: "May Hashem grant you the vision to see the presence of G-d in your world."

It is a mimeged blessing. She shouldn't bear the presence of G-d. The price is too high – if I even suffered from such a weight. But she should see it in others. She should know it. Because those who recognize the presence of G-d in others are necessary to bring it to our reality. They are the heaven to dew, the sun to grain, the moon to children.

I continue, "May Hashem bless you and keep you, may He make his face shine upon you and be gracious to you and may He lift His face to you and may he grant you peace."

And then I withdraw my hands. I will die soon, and all will be lost. But perhaps my child will carry *something* forward.

Perhaps all is not in vain.

Then Chaya raises her head and she looks at me.

143

Her eyes are wide with surprise and shock and confusion and, yes, with joy.

In that moment, I know she is seeing the presence of G-d; in me.

In that moment I know, even as I am slow dying in that mental institution, that all will be well.

The Torah reading of *V'ZOT HABERACHA* is the final Torah reading. It records the death of Moshe and the final blessings he gives the people. The reading opens with a remarkable juxtaposition. Moshe is called, for the only time, *'ISH HAELOKIM'* – the 'man of G-d'. And the verses that follow open up confusion. *HASHEM OMER MISINAI BAH...* It is a verse we translate as "[Moshe] said, G-d came from Sinai." But a more straight-forward reading is that G-d is speaking "Hashem said, [Moshe] came from Sinai." It is unclear who is speaking – the greatest of prophets or G-d himself.

What follows is a series of blessings. One for each tribe but Shimon. G-d promises thousands of generations of kindness to those who love him. And Moshe, the great protector, shares that kindness with us. But Moshe's blessings have not been fulfilled. They are promises from G-d Almighty for the tribes of the people of Israel. But today, the tribes no longer exist.

Yisrael, the man in this story, is identifying them once again. He is preparing them for the blessing of Moshe. He is of the tribe of Yosef, not delivering salvation – but a necessary, indirect, contributor to it. He is fulfilling that most beautiful of Moshe's blessings.

At the end of the reading, when Hashem shows Moshe the land, he doesn't show a place of Canaanites and Jebusites. He shows him a place of Dan and Naftali and Ephraim and Menashe. He shows him the future.

144

And Moshe knows, as he leaves the people who troubled him so, that they will be blessed. He knows that all will not be for naught.

"And there hath not arisen a prophet since in Israel like unto Moshe, whom the LORD knew face to face;"

May we live the vision of Moshe, the Man of G-d.

And may we dance with joy; celebrating the timeless blessings of our people.

Rosh Hashanah: Globus Corp

I felt like a little girl in a wonderland when I showed up for my first day at work. I had gone to one of the most sophisticated and modern colleges in the country. Most classes were held off-site, but when you did visit what you saw was a hyper-modern campus. There were grass-covered buildings, curving glass walls and wide-open internal 'teamwork' spaces. Any new fad or design concept was completely integrated into the learning experience.

I loved *learning* there, but I didn't want to *work* in that sort of place.

No, since childhood I'd had my eyes on another company: the Legacy Tooling Corporation.

I know it sounds weird, working for a tooling company. My parents thought I was nuts. But I was an engineer – basically from birth – and making things *to help others make things* always seemed tremendously exciting to me. Plus, Legacy Tooling wasn't quite like other companies. They basically lived off a single large customer: Globus Corp. Now, before you get visions of some faceless multinational corporation, consider this: Globus makes pretty much everything. No, scratch that, *Globus makes everything.*

And Legacy makes their tooling.

Incredibly, Legacy's founders somehow got an exclusive deal with Globus. Other people could supply other things, but their tooling would come from *us*.

146

There I go with the *us*. Even on that first day, I thought of Legacy as *my* company. I didn't just work there; I was an integral part of the place and it was a part of me.

Now Legacy wasn't located in some new building in a new neighborhood. No, they'd built their headquarters, generations before, in one of the oldest neighborhoods there was. The building had *legacy* written all over it. It was grand, it was Ivy covered. It practically screamed for respect. Go new-fangled all you want, but the dressing on that edifice said something even my university couldn't: this place has got some history.

When I got inside, I continued to be bedazzled. The place was a buzz of activity. The engineers around me were working on some of the coolest things I'd ever seen. I walked through lab after lab and was just blown away by what they were putting together. Everything reinforced my belief that I'd made the right choice. Not that it was really a choice.

I got put on a team designing a doohickey. I'll call it that, because I can barely even describe what it was. It was just a doohickey. Well, to be completely honest and to put it technically: *it was a really amazing doohickey.*

My group was awesome. At our daily standups, we'd update everybody on our progress and then we'd end it with a circle of appreciations and a group clap. We were so excited about what we were doing. And we were good at it. And we loved each other.

And then, during one planning meeting, I turned to the group (awesome engineers all, I can tell you) and asked: "How's Globus gonna use this thing?"

They just stared back at me. Then they got back to work. It was weird... I took a gander at the requirements and I realized that they basically consisted of "make something really cool, and it'll be cool." Globus wasn't even mentioned.

I didn't ask the question again. I didn't want to make waves. I didn't want to lose my job. I loved the place. But the question kept asking me; if you know what I mean. I'd look around at project after product and wonder "How is Globus gonna use *that* doohickey?"

And I never had an answer. It was like our engineering and manufacturing groups had incredible people turning out incredible stuff – but they had no connection to the actual customer.

And then I began to notice the first cracks in the business. They started literally. I mean, the subbasement in that old place had concrete that was beginning to serious deteriorate. I looked into it and learned that while the building had been Legacy's old headquarters, they'd had some *very* lean times and Globus had only recently repurchased their building for them.

Legacy wasn't taking care of the building through. I thought it was because nobody was paying attention to it. But it turned out *everybody* was paying attention to it. The problem was that it was a very particular building. Globus had built it (of course) and only Globus had the tools necessary to fix it.

And for some reason, Globus was letting it crumble.

This stunned me.

I kept snooping around – both physically and via the IT network – and I learned more and more. The scariest thing I learned was that Globus wasn't using what we were making.

We were just making cool stuff. But it was stuff that didn't serve our customer.

I was like "what the heck is going on here?" I looked into the sales group, wondering whether they were just dropping the ball. I thought about printing myself another badge and physically sneaking around the place. But I learned something downright weird. *Everybody* in sales was a guy. A badge wouldn't have done me much good.

I could learn things anyway; computer networks are fun. Anyway, the sales group had an enormous number of sales meetings. They had pretty much every weekend reserved for some get together or another. But they also met during the week... wait for it... *several times a day*. And they didn't meet at the office; they had meals at local watering holes and restaurants and function halls *all the time*.

I took lunch one day, headed out and took a seat next to one of the sales meetings. It was even weirder than the engineering group was. The sales guys (all guys, remember) were sitting there, jabbering away. They were praising Globus and begging and pleading for revenue. They weren't even talking about our products. It was like the products were irrelevant to the conversation.

And the Globus reps? The Globus reps just looked like – well, you know when you're at a party and somebody starts talking to you and they won't shut up and they ignore pretty much every cue you send at them and you can't get away? Yeah, the Globus reps looked like that. Occasionally, they tried to get a word in edgewise, but our sales guys were so busy talking they barely heard them. One time, they listened – but then they took the Globus guy's words and *totally* reinterpreted them. They made them reinforce the annoying speech they'd been given before. They turned them into praise for their approach to sales. You've had that happen before, right? You say "go away" to the guy at the party and he thinks you're just encouraging him to do more of what he's already doing because it is so clearly working. Right?

Ugh.

I have to say, seeing that, that I was kind of freaking out. I mean, who hires these people. Yeah, so I looked into that too and I worked out that almost all my co-workers were lifers. They were smart, don't get me wrong, but they had spent their whole lives with the company. And I mean that. Almost all of them had *parents* who worked there. Lifers+. Can you imagine that, in this day and age?

I began to get scared then. But if Globus stopped paying us whatever Globus was paying us, Legacy would get shellacked. And there'd be carnage. Our employees wouldn't be able to find work anywhere. They'd never done anything *useful*.

Legacy had sales and production – but the darned things weren't connected to the customer. It was like the company itself had no identity. It had no life. Just a building and great people (well, except for those sales guys – but I was sure even they could learn).

I decided to do something about it.

Problem was, I didn't know what. People thought I was weird when I asked production about the customer. I couldn't imagine what sales would think when I asked them about production. They had *no* connection. It was like one group wouldn't even acknowledge the other group existed.

But I had to do something, right? So, I put together this evaluation matrix (I am a production engineer, after all) and I marked it whenever a production guy (or gal) actually had the customer in mind when they designed something. I marked it whenever a sales guy (never mind the gal bit) actually helped production know what the customer wanted. I marked it whenever a sales guy actually *talked* to production. I mean, our customer was a *manufacturer*. You wanna get to know them, start in-house. So, I made a little list – a *really* little list – but in my book it was a list of *honor*. These were the guys (and gals) who were doing it right.

Legacy needed them. I mean, we were living off old contracts. We were living pretty well, but from what I'd seen, Globus could pull most of those contracts at any moment and things were literally cracking anyway.

I told a few people about my list, and I got a few more people involved in keeping it up. But it was still pretty much a secret. I was scared. I mean, who was *I*? I was surrounded by lifer's+ and I was trying to tell them how to run *their* company? Don't get me wrong, there was a lot of that. The old guard – in any part of the company – was darned good at circling their wagons and totally excluding somebody who poked holes in what they were doing. I mean, they were *awesome* at it. When they turned their guns on you it was like getting excommunicated.

But I kept quiet. I didn't get excommunicated. I just kept my little list.

Then, inevitably, more cracks began to appear. The roof was literally leaking (not good when dealing with some pretty touchy materials). We tried to patch it up, but the job was imperfect. People started worrying. I mean, they'd only moved back in a little while ago. They'd had some really lean times. And now, not long into things, the situation is getting pretty tough again. They remembered, like *really remembered*, when things were horrifyingly terrible. I don't think I can find adjectives to describe the things they told me about.

So, *they* began to worry. All sorts of people began to suggest ideas of how to fix things. Not just the building, but the business. Sales people wanted *all* of production to join them in begging Globus for more revenue. Production guys wanted to fire everybody in sales and just start making as much stuff as they could.

I just sat there, flabbergasted.

I was scared, really scared. I figured they might beat me up or kick me out – but I knew that if Legacy fell apart, so did I. I was a part of them. Lifer+ or not, there was no escaping it. I decided to do a Queen Esther and put myself out there.

It was simple. I began to share my list. My little cohort of friends began to heap honor on the people who were on it. We didn't argue the idea behind the list, we just praised the production people who had the customer in mind and the sales guys who brought production and the customer together. We made it an honor to serve the customer, in every part of the organization. It was that simple. And, amazingly, it worked. Sure, there was some fierce resistance. I mean a whole lot of our engineers just wanted to make cool stuff and a whole lot of our sales guys just wanted long weekends with the customer.

But soon most people began to realize my way was working.

Production folks discovered they *liked* making stuff that got used. It validated them. It gave them, not to be too hokey about it, *meaning*. The salespeople discovered they *liked* actually having a customer who was interested in what they had to offer. They liked helping the production people give the customer what they wanted. The sales guys (and even a few gals then) began to realize that production was why they were there. It helped them relate to the customer who was, after all, a manufacturer. And the production guys began to realize that sales were why they were there.

They weren't just there to make stuff. They were there to make stuff so the sales guys could get it to the customer.

The new ideas swept through the whole organization. Everything got calibrated around Globus. No longer was Globus some unheard of and unmentioned entity in production – now it was core to everything.

Of course, I got promoted. No, scratch that, I got *PROMOTED*. I was made like Chief Muckymuck of the whole company. I gotta say, that was cool.

And then the revenues started pouring in. Globus fixed up the building.

Things were awesome. And they are *still* awesome.

It turns out we're *really* good at selling to Globus. Before, even though Globus built literally *everything*, not everybody knew about them. But our success opened up a whole lot of eyes. Soon, lots of other companies began to come to us and we began tying *them* into our sales channels. We began to help them connect with Globus.

I mean, it was awesome.

I take that back. It *is* awesome.

And all of it was so *simple* that even a little geek of a girl who went to some fancy new-age university could understood what had to happen.

This story is not about Globus and Legacy. It is about Hashem and the Jewish people. The woman at the center of the story, is, naturally, a *ger* (convert).

If you talk about the nation of Israel, *our* customer is Hashem. But we do a terrible job of selling to Him. We have our old headquarters back, but we're pretty dysfunctional. Our roof has holes (rockets) and our ground (with dry ground and tunnels) is cracking.

We all propose different solutions without realizing that we just have to put our solutions together.

It is that simple. Our sales people have to understand G-d is the *Creator*. They don't have to create themselves; they just need to appreciate and honor the act of creation while helping those who do create apply their creation to our relationship with the customer. They don't need revenue (*PARNASSAH*), they need creation and holiness (the use of creation for the timeless relationship). They need to bring our national product to G-d. On the other hand, our production guys, who are *creators*, need to actually create for a purpose – connection to G-d.

All of this is in the Torah: G-d is the Creator and we connect to him through Offerings (*KORBANOT*) which are literally 'closenesses'. What can we bring as *KORBANOT*? Only things we had a part in making. No wild animals or fruit. Just our crops and domesticated flocks. The Kohanim don't make anything, but they facilitate the transaction. They exist to connect production with the customer. They actually obviate themselves as individuals in the process. They are simply middlemen.

This is the Torah reality. We are supposed to be the world's example of creation with a purpose. We are supposed to waste as little potential as possible (*TUMAH*). But for now, despite having our old headquarters back, we lack a national identity build around serving the customer. Everything is disconnected. As I put it in a recent sermon:

As a nation, we engage in the cycle of creation and rest with the Divine – but we don't do it with intent. Instead, some resent creation and cherish holiness while others resent holiness and cherish creation.

Rosh Hashana is a great time to think about fixing this. If we serve our national customer – if we find it an honor to serve Him (or Her, depending on context) – then He (or She) will reward us.

That's our highest goal this Rosh Hashana.

Think about it.

And then come back to me.

Maybe we can start putting together a list.

Yom Kippur: The Man in the Cab

I looked at the man sharing the back seat of the cab with me. He was my age, and he looked almost exactly like me. The similarities were incredible; the chances seemed infinitesimal.

How did I end up in *this* cab, with *this* man?

Just a few minutes earlier, I'd paused to admire the beauty of downtown Sydney, Australia. Not the harbor or the bridge or the Opera House. No, what had attracted my eye was the contrast between the brand-new, shining glass and steel towers, and the incredible sandstone edifice occupied by the Industrial Relations Commission. The sun was glinting off the modern glass towers, the rush of cars was filling my ears and the faint scent of salted air was touching my nose. Then the sky suddenly darkened, and rain started pelting the street around me.

I had a flight to catch, and I didn't want to needlessly ruin my suit. So, I flagged down a cab. A man next to me was trying to do the same. But I knew cabs would be hard to come by.

"Where are you headed?" I asked.

The man was covering part of his head with a newspaper; I hadn't seen one of those in a while.

"Airport," he said. He had a clear American accent. He was no local. Neither was I.

"I am too," I answered, "Let's share a cab."

"Okay."

Moments later, one of those big four-door Ford sedans you can only find in Australia pulled to the curb. We both slipped into the back seat. The city seemed to have vanished: the shards of light gone, the sounds of the city muted and the smell of the ocean water replaced by the scent of plastic seats. Only after I settled in did I look up.

Sitting next to me was my doppelganger. The only difference seemed to be that he had a short beard and was wearing jeans and a loose-fitting button-down shirt. Otherwise, we could have been identical twins.

I didn't know what else to do, so I stuck out my hand.

"Nick," I said. He grasped it firmly.

"Jon," he said. At least we didn't share a name.

"Where to?" asked the cabbie.

"Airport," we answered, together.

Moments later, we got moving. And moments after that, the traffic closed around us. It had formed as quickly as the rain clouds. I hadn't factored this in, there was a chance I'd miss my flight.

It'd be an appropriate end to a frustrating trip from the States.

There was nothing to do about it now though. So, I turned to my seatmate. "What brings you to Sydney?" I asked. My wife was a little embarrassed by my willingness to talk to total strangers, but I loved learning about people.

Jon smiled back at me, "Writing, actually."

"You're a writer?" I asked.

He nodded.

I used to write, a long while back.

"How'd you get into that?" I asked.

"You want the long version or the short one?"

I look at the flooded streets and the unmoving cars. "I'll take the long one," I said.

"Well, it isn't that long," said the man, "I wrote a lot, back in college. After I graduated, I got a job as a tech writer. But I kept up my creative writing. My mother kept telling me to keep at it, and then *something* would pop. So, I did. In every free moment, I wrote. I got married after a few years and slowed down a bit. But I kept writing. The thing was, *nothing* popped. Nobody was reading my stuff. I'd get like three hits on one of my short pieces and that was it."

"That doesn't fund a trip to Sydney," I said.

"No, it doesn't." he answered, "I was going to give up. I had other things to do. But my wife picked up my mother's drumbeat. 'Keep going,' she said, 'It'll work, eventually.' But eventually, her enthusiasm wasn't enough for me. I mean, I'd contacted agents but they didn't want to hear from a random guy like me. I felt bad even reaching out. They were flooded by people; how were they supposed to know my stuff was any good, right?"

I nodded.

"And then," Jon said, "I was in an airport security line and the lady behind me looked particularly frazzled. The line wasn't going anywhere, so I asked 'tough day?' And she began to tell me about her day. She was a literary agent. She'd been at a conference. And people had been pestering her all day. She said she was on *the toilet* and people were trying to get her to read their work. It sounded crazy. I didn't want to bother her, but I asked what she was looking for – just to be polite. She told me. It happened that I had something that fit, to a T, on my phone. But I didn't want to show it to her. She'd been pestered on the toilet, after all. I didn't need to make the line worse than the TSA already had. Then she asked, 'do you write?' and I said yes. And she *asked* to see something. And I showed her that piece and she was smitten."

"What happened next?" I asked, genuinely curious.

"It turned out she'd always wanted to be an agent. Since she was a kid. She was *really* good at networking and at determining what could work and what couldn't. And she *loved* what I'd written. She read it right there in the security line. Before we got to the end of that line, she emailed me a contract. And she took it from there. She took that one short story and pitched it to an online network. And that *one* short story became a five-season TV series. It made her career, and mine. Ever since, I've been writing."

"Wow," I said, genuinely impressed.

"I used to write," I said, "I used to be a technical writer too."

"What happened?" asked Jon.

"I gave it up," I said, "It wasn't going anywhere, just like with you. I started using my spare time another way."

"How?"

"It started after I got married. I was a process manager in a large company. But at night, I used to visit investor and small business conferences. I wasn't an investor and I wasn't trying to raise money. I just thought I could be helpful and it'd be a great chance to network. I helped people do pro-formas and write business plans and such. Then my wife and I had kids and my time kind of dried up. But we had a few challenges along the way. It was the usual: getting them to sleep, moderating their behavior, all that kind of basic stuff."

"I get that," Jon said, "I've got five kids myself."

"Me too," I said, surprised to hear he had as many as I did. "Anyway, we had these friends who seemed to have it all under control. The mother especially. We asked them for advice. It worked, totally. My wife started calling the mother her 'mentor.' She consulted with her regularly and the woman was really good with her advice. Then I had an idea. Maybe they could start a little club-based business, like Weight Watchers, but for parenting. It could do a lot of people a lot of good. I helped them put together a business plan and all that and I introduced them to some angel investors. It all went so incredibly well. They now have chapters all over the world, with mentors and milestones and all that. And, as a thank you, they gave me 5% of the company."

"Are you still a process manager?"

"No," I answered, with a smile, "I'm in finance now. I invest specifically in what I call skills businesses; businesses that teach people life skills like cooking, personal finance, time management and so on. I get to empower people and make a living all at the same time."

"So, what brought you to Oz?"

"I'm looking for opportunities. I'm an investor myself now, on a pretty big scale. But I don't want to sit on my coattails. I can help people. So, I came here looking for things to invest in."

"Any success?" asked Jon.

I shook my head, 'no.'

"What are you here for?" I asked.

"Funny enough," said Jon, "Finance. But not for a skills business. I want to finance a movie, based on a book I wrote about the Middle East."

"Any luck?" I asked.

"None," Jon answered, "The people I met with weren't interested."

"Why not?" I asked.

"The book's a bit odd," Jon answered, "It isn't just entertainment. It is about showing a path to a better reality. It's about creating an environment where people can learn a new way of doing things."

"So, a skills business, of sorts."

Jon smiled, "I guess so, yes."

"Do you have a copy?"

Jon grinned and pulled a tome from his bag.

"I won't be able to finish it on the cab ride," I said.

"If you read the first two chapters and you like it, you can keep it." Jon said.

So, I opened the book and started reading. It grabbed me at once. And I knew that this was something I wanted to finance. I fell into the book. It was amazing. We'd both come to Sydney to meet with other people. Or at least, we thought we had. But in fact, we'd actually come to Sydney to meet one another.

Suddenly, I heard a sharp voice. "Sir, Sir!"

It was the cabbie. I snapped open my eyes. They'd been shut? And then I looked towards Jon. I didn't mean to fall asleep reading his book. It was insulting.

But the cab was empty.

"Did the other guy leave?" I asked the cabbie.

"No other guy," he answered, in a Filipino accent, "We're here."

And we were. The departures terminal was outside my window.

Hurriedly, I pulled my credit card from my wallet. But it didn't say 'Nick.' It said 'Joseph.'

I handed it to the driver, confused. But he didn't notice. He just gave me my receipt and helped me with my bags as I stepped out of the cab.

Then it hit me. I wasn't Nick and I wasn't Jon. I'd come here for a job interview. It had gone well. The job represented a great opportunity. But I wasn't Nick or Jon. I wasn't an author with a chance to change the world or an international financier who specialized in helping people deal with everyday problems.

I wasn't Nick or Jon.

But I had been them, hadn't I? I'd been a tech writer who wrote on the side. I'd met that literary agent in the security line, but I'd had nothing to show her – I'd taken a pause in my writing. I'd met the couple who were so good at raising children, but I had no investors to connect them with.

I hadn't maximized the use of my free time. Certainly, I hadn't been hurting anybody. But while I had been successful and I had been blessed with a beautiful family, I hadn't accomplished *all* that I could have.

I'd been both Nick and Jon, I realized, but I'd become neither.

As I made my way through the airport, a tinge of regret threatened to swallow me up.

But I knew, somehow, that I'd have another chance.

The centerpiece of YOM KIPPUR is the ritual of AZ-AZEL. In that ritual, one goat is dedicated to the timeless relationship with G-d. That goat represents our creative and holy actions. The other is dedicated to AZ-AZEL, which literally means 'Goat of Disappearance'. Our sins are placed on it, and they vanish as if they never existed.

Sometimes these sins are acts of destruction. Sometimes they leave a hole that can take generations before it is filled in. In a way, YOM KIPPUR enables us to accelerate that process.

But not all sins are destructive.

Some sins are only a failure to take advantage of blessings. Blessings, whether health, money, talent or chance meetings, are simply opportunities. But if we aren't ready for those opportunities, then the things we *could have done* vanish without ever existing. These sins vanish like the stories of Nick and Jon; they exist only as day dreams of what might have been.

In our lives, we can only take one path. We can't be *both* Nick and Jon. But if we fail to work and prepare ourselves for opportunity, then *we can be neither.*

To twist the Field of Dreams: "If you don't build it, they'll never come."

I have a very recent example of this. Last Shabbat's story, the Barn, almost didn't exist. In a normal year, the reading of VAYEILECH would have been combined with the one for the week before. I already had a story for the week before, and so I didn't *need* to write one for VAYEILECH.

But, at the urging of my wife, I *did* write a story. It is already the third most popular story on my website. More importantly, I had a chance to honor a friend's father and provide my friend some small measure of comfort in his time of mourning.

But it *almost didn't exist.* A bit of laziness and neither that story nor the man in the cab from that story (who forms the inspiration for this story) would have existed.

That is the kind of sin that does not need to be cast into oblivion, because it never emerges from it.

This is the sin I am doing teshuva (repentance) for this year. I am doing teshuva for the opportunities I will never know about because I was not ready for them. Today, I know I am missing opportunities because my Hebrew is so poor. That lack locks me out of relationships with huge swaths of the country I live in. And my traditional Jewish learning is similarly bereft, robbing me of depth that I could use to benefit those around me.

As is tradition in a *YOM KIPPUR* greeting, I ask you to forgive me if I have sinned against you. And, I grant the same forgiveness to all of you, whether or not I am aware of your infractions.

In this way, I hope you are erasing my sins just as I am erasing yours.

But we should all remember erasure, oblivion, is a sad substitute for eternity. We should all remember that *YOM KIPPUR* represents not only an end to past regrets, but the beginnings of a new reality.

And so, I want to end with a blessing.

Please G-d, in the coming year, may we all find opportunities to use our time more productively. It is up to us to take them. Perhaps then, in a virtuous cycle, we will be able to bring new realities and opportunities into existence – for ourselves and for others.

Then, together, we will continually grow in our connection to the timeless Divine.

May you be inscribed in the Book of Life

Sukkot: The Contraband

You can imagine a generic suburban bar, trying to be cool and grungy, right? You have the spotless floors done up in some dirty-looking pattern. You have mass-manufactured memorabilia lining the walls. Memorabilia which is identical to that on every other wall in the entire chain. You have the smell of food that isn't really too greasy filling the air. And, most importantly, you have the people. They aren't grungy or beat up. They are safely middle-class: clean, drug-free, well-fed and well-dressed.

You can imagine that, right?

This wasn't that place.

I was downtown, but I wasn't in the classy part of downtown. Instead, I was on a stage in the worst bar I'd ever seen. The floors were genuinely dirty and there were no memorabilia on the walls. The place smelled like a mix of mold, sugary soda, body odor, and urine. It made its money on the cover charge: $3 to get in. The 'guests' were paying for access to the bathrooms. Just not as bathrooms. They were really paying for a place to shoot up. You could see it in their eyes as they emerged from the stalls; tiny pupils revealed the freshly deposited opiates in their bloodstreams. In a unique twist, there wasn't even alcohol on tap. The place had to be able to welcome all ages. Homeless parents didn't want to leave their kids outside while they did drugs in the bathrooms. They loved their kids, and so they brought them in.

The place had live music. They didn't pay the acts much; they weren't the point. They were only there so the clientele could shuffle like zombies in the back of the room and the management could

165

pretend they weren't just a clearing house for those buying and selling illicit substances. Of course, it was all done with a wink. After all, the place was called The Contraband.

They had to keep up the front, though. So, they had music. And, that night, the music was me.

I was a violist of all things. Not a violinist, a violist. I went to college for it. I graduated with honors. I had perfect technique. I was almost robotic in my capabilities. I'd tried to make a career out of it. My parents thought I was ridiculous. I came from one of those firmly middle-class backgrounds. I was supposed to become a professional of some sort; a respectable woman. I certainly wasn't meant to end up in a place like this.

But I had ended up here. And the reason was simple: I didn't have a *voice*. I could play a mean viola, and I could play pretty much any genre. But all I had was technique. I didn't have any soul. That's why, after I graduated from college, I had to do everything I could for a gig. I played alternative viola in those middle-class bars. I played country viola (just think of a deep fiddle) in the country. Then I lost even those gigs; I didn't fire people's imaginations. Now I was playing punk viola – my instrument shouting at the room – in places like these.

In the classier places, people would talk about my technique. Even here, at The Contraband, they'd come out of their stupor long enough to ask me where I'd learned how to play. But nobody ever said I *spoke to them* through my music. I was just a touch of light entertainment. A robot could have done what I was doing.

That was why I knew, when men talked to me, that they weren't interested in my music. When men in a place like this talked to me, they scared me. Not that The Contraband was unique in that way. I couldn't trust any of the men I met when I worked. When I was working the middle-class bars, the men tended to be married. And here? Here, they tended to be dangerous.

That night was different. That night, I was thrashing my viola. And, sitting in the back of the room, was a skeleton of a man nursing a soda bought from the skeleton of a 'dry' bar. He was thin, desperately thin. His glasses were way out of fashion. His clothes were cheap, ill-fitting and old. Not like he was poor, but like he didn't care about how others saw him.

He was staring at me.

I hadn't noticed him at first. At first, he'd blended into the crowd. When I did, I couldn't take my eyes off of him. He was enthralled by me and I was enthralled by him. After the set, he didn't come up to me, and I didn't go to him. When I finished for the night, he just wasn't there. He'd vanished completely. I asked others about him, but nobody had noticed that he was there.

I had an offer for another gig, in another place, a few days later. It was a step up (it was hard for anything to be anything other than a step up). But The Contraband wanted me too. I was good cover – punk viola made it look like they were about the music. I decided, there and then, to go back. I wanted to see that skeleton of a man.

I started my act and then, at some point, I looked up and he was there again. Staring at me just like he had before. He was frightening in his intensity. I knew I should have avoided him. But I couldn't help myself. After my set I walked up to him and I asked him who he was. And he just looked at me. I could see something strange in his eyes. There was fear. And there was, could it be, love? He was wrestling with himself, trying to decide what to do. And then he turned to the bar, and scribbled something down on a piece of paper. He handed it to me and I took it. Then he got up, wordlessly, and just walked out.

I looked at the paper, confused. There were three shorts lines on it. An address.

The creepy skeleton of a man in the bar had given me an address.

Any sensible person would probably have burned the thing. They probably would have stopped playing this sort of venue and found another career. But I couldn't do that. I stuffed the address in my pocket and I went back to playing. Over the next few days, I played the encounter through my head again and again. What did the man want? What was he up to? Was he dangerous?

I looked up the address.

Google Earth revealed the place was a shack surrounded by tall grass and abandoned lots in a part of town that was actually crappier than The Contraband itself. It wasn't the sort of place I should visit. It wasn't that I was a middle-class girl. Even a woman 'in the trade' knew better than to go to abandoned buildings to visit strange men who handed them addresses in the backs of places like The Contraband.

Two weeks passed. I played at The Contraband every chance I got, but *he* wasn't there. The address burned in my pocket, filling me with questions and a strange kind of yearning I couldn't quite place. I had to see the man again. I had to understand why he had given me that address.

One day, I gave in.

It was stupid. But I had to see him again, and I had to understand. I took the bus to the worst part of town. For some reason, I took my viola with me. When I got off the bus, the streets were basically empty. It was a threatening absence, like attackers could emerge from anywhere at any time. You could smell the grasses and the faint odor of the dangerous men who had been here not long before me. For that moment, I was grateful for my own poor clothes. Except for the viola, I didn't look like a target.

I walked down the street – past derelict buildings and falling houses and empty lots overgrown with glass bottles and grass. I came to the address he had given me. It looked abandoned. There was a chain link fence around it. Somebody had cut some of the links. There was a shack in the middle of the lot, barely held together and patched with blue plastic tarps.

There were no windows.

I sucked in a huge breath and then shimmied through the fence, crossed the rough ground and came up to the door of the shack itself. I paused, and then I knocked on the door. It swung open, on creaking hinges. It was dark inside; there was no electricity. There was a faint smell of the rotted wood planking that held the place together. And there was a faint blue glow, cast by the tarps that covered the shack's poorly joined corners.

I should have stopped then, but I didn't. I pushed the door all the way open and I walked inside.

It took my eyes a little while to adjust. Then I saw him. The man. He was sitting in the corner, on a plastic chair. He looked at me, that combination of fear and love in his eyes.

I looked at him, realizing I somehow felt the same way.

He began to sing.

I don't know how to describe what I heard in that broken-down shack. It was harsh and biting and discordant. But at the same time, it was the most intensely beautiful thing I have ever encountered. The walls seemed to echo with the love and mercy *and power* of that man's voice. I didn't hear any words, just notes. Notes that seemed to be piled one on top of the other like unwashed plates after a family meal, or like layers of silt in a running stream, or like books that have been lovingly consumed by a voracious reader.

It seemed like I would drift away in that music. By the sadness, by the joy, by the wisdom contained within those notes. The man touched my hand, bringing me back. He kept singing.

I watched him, I watched his face. He was illuminated by his wordless song.

It seemed like all the world was in that voice. It seemed like you could disappear into the vastness of what he sang. I knew his song was rebuilding me from the inside out.

Then, he was done.

The place was silent. There were just the two of us, standing there, looking at one another with something far closer to love than to fear. I wanted to ask why he didn't perform. I wanted to ask why he wasn't on stage. When he let go of my hand, I knew the answer.

Most people couldn't hear that music and stay themselves. They would drift away, as I almost had. I realized what his fear had been – it was fear that I wouldn't have been able to hear his music. He had kept me there, with the touch of his fingertips. Without his touch, I could have vanished, happily erased within the beauty of his voice.

We didn't speak, even then. But his music became a part of me.

I knew why he had brought me there.

I left then. We still hadn't exchanged a single snippet of conversation. But we had shared so much more.

I went back to The Contraband. But now *my* music was different. I had *his* music inside of me. I played and watched the zombies turn and pull themselves back into reality. I touched them. I touched their souls. When my set ended, they just stood there, eagerly waiting for more. I got other opportunities then. I played in other places. And I changed people everywhere I went. I thought about making a record or an mp3. But, somehow, I knew *this* music wasn't meant for records. It had to be transmitted in person – person to person. You had to be there to feel it.

I played larger and larger venues. I laminated that old address and I wore it like a necklace. Tucked under my blouse. It was a constant reminder of the risk I had taken. Overnight, it seemed like I became a sensation. You couldn't listen to my tunes on the radio or on YouTube. You had to come and listen, in person.

I was the modern artist who did nothing modern.

I knew *he* was behind my music. Others sensed it as well. He had given me a spirit and I had given him a voice. Everybody knew that I was expressing the soul of another artist. I was okay with that, for a time. I was touching their souls. Every so often, I would even go back to that shack, and I would listen to the voice of a man I knew better than any other.

I became more and more successful. But then, somehow, I began to believe *I* was responsible for *my* success. It began to anger me that I was simply channeling *his* music.

I wanted my own voice. I wanted to get out from under the thumb of the skeleton of a man.

And so, almost as if I was rebelling against his rule, I shut out his music. I tried to find my own voice, borrowing from the genres that surrounded me. I went back to the punk viola and the rock viola and the pop viola.

But nothing had any traction.

My music had no life. As hard as I tried, it had no soul. People left my shows, disappointed. I climbed back down the ladder of success. I realized my mistake, of course. But it was too late.

When I tried to play *his* music once again, it was gone.

There was a void where his love had once been.

I even went back to the shack, again and again. But it was always empty.

It seemed like nobody had ever been living there.

I was cursed again, playing The Contraband. Drug addicts asked me where I learned my technique.

Nobody was touched by what *my* music had to say.

And then, one evening, in that drug-infested venue, I had a revelation. It wasn't that I suddenly realized my music had no soul, I'd known that before. And it wasn't that I suddenly realized that my music offered no chance of success or fame; I'd already figured that out.

No, I knew, in that instance, that *my music* was destined to vanish. I played it and it disappeared almost as soon as the notes left my bow. It was like I was playing a melody, and it was consumed by a waiting void.

I wanted to cry then. I knew there was another path. The man's voice might not have been *mine* alone, but it was the voice *I* was meant to have. The music he gave me flew off my bow, resonating through the deep cavities of my viola and seemed to fill the space around me. *His* notes seemed to stay within those who heard them, a timeless after-effect that gave meaning to my life and to the lives of those who heard me.

His was the music of eternity and he had chosen me to play it.

In that instant, I felt *his* music once again. I began to play *his* music once again. And I was filled with joy at the opportunity. It wasn't about fame or money. It was about giving reality to something far greater than I could ever be.

I played that music. I closed my eyes and I imagined myself back in that shack. I heard his voice within me and I shared it with the world around me. The zombies stopped and pulled themselves back into reality. I kept playing, imagining the music spinning out, far beyond the walls of The Contraband. I imagined it touching the bums in the street, the police in their cars, the suburbanites in their suburban houses and the couples gazing out over the slowly moving downtown river.

I imagined that music filling the world. I imagined the beauty it could bring.

Then I opened my eyes and *he* was there, just like the first time. He was watching me from the 'dry' bar. His eyes were full of forgiveness. And his eyes were full of love. There was no fear.

I felt the tears streaming from my eyes. Tears of joy and tears of longing and tears of regret as I remembered what I had abandoned in service of my pride.

I knew then that he was my soul and I was his voice.

And I kept playing, the laminated address resting underneath my blouse.

I knew I had to keep playing. I knew I had to bring his music to the world.

I watched the skeleton of a man smile.

And I wondered, just for a moment, if he was really there.

We just emerged from Yom Kippur. The centerpiece of that festival is the offering of *AZ-AZEL*. There are two goats in that offering. Both represent the Jewish people. But one is dedicated to our timeless relationship with G-d. The other is dedicated to *AZ-AZEL*, the goat of disappearance. The lesson is this: we can be dedicated to G-d and connect with the timeless or we can follow another path and disappear as if we never existed.

The action represents the moment of *KAPARAH* – of sealing ourselves against the spiritual rot of the world. It is the moment of forgiveness and the moment of repair. We listen to the shofar, hearing the shadow of the voice of G-d, and then we recognize that all else is vanity – and we return to Hashem.

But what have we returned to? Is it wealth? Is it success? What are we seeking?

The answer comes with Sukkot. Sukkot has three prominent features.

The first is the *ARBA'AT HAMINIM* (the four species). They represent the strength of our relationship with G-d. The first, *PRI ETZ HADAR* means 'fruit of a beautiful tree'. Trees are Divine blessing. The most beautiful tree is the covenant with G-d. And the Torah is its fruit. The second, *ANAF EITZ AVOT* is also a gift from G-d (as indicated by the *EITZ*, or tree). *ANAF* appears nowhere else in Chumash – it is mysterious. *AVOT* (with an *EYIN*) is used to describe the gold (Divine) braid that surrounds and connects the stones with the names of the tribes of Israel on the Kohen's clothes. The *ANAF EITZ AVOT* thus represents Hashem's mysterious desire to embrace us. The third, *KAPOT TEMARIM* are 'palms of *TAMARIM*'. Palms hold things and hands represent action. Tamar, the daughter-in-law of Yehuda, took her life into her own hands to be a part of the people. Her palms thus represent our desire to be with Hashem. And *ARVEI NACHAL* is the 'brook willow'. It can also literally mean 'mixed stream.' We are G-d's *NACHAL* – spreading His spiritual waters and mixing the human and the Divine. *ARVEI NACHAL* represents our gift to Him.

These four species represent G-d's gift to the Jewish people, our gift to Him and our mutual desire to be together. We wave the representation of that relationship, and we celebrate with G-d.

This is represented in the story by the playing of the music (the mutual gift) and by the laminated tag – a reminder of the risks the violist took to be with the singer and of his mysterious embrace of her.

The second feature is the timeless 'Sukkah' we stayed in when we first left our exile. That is the shack where we dwelt with Hashem and heard His music for the first time.

The third feature is the offerings. We bring offerings, but not just on our own behalf. We bring offerings on behalf of the nations. We bring the nations to G-d and G-d to the nations – just as the violist does when playing the final set of the story.

Of course, we have not finished this task. So, the offerings represent not just our mutual relationship, but the incompleteness of our gift to him.

For me the lesson is clear: we have returned to G-d, but a tremendous effort remains before us. In the year to come, we must find ways to play the music of our G-d to the world. It is our gift, it is our responsibility – and it is the core of our being.

Hashem may not be sitting before us, but He remains within us. He is our soul, and we are His voice.

Author's Note

The Biblical Joseph was given *useful* interpretations when he gave credit to Hashem for his understanding. He finally gave full credit to G-d when he said:

בלעדי: אלקים יענה

"It is not in me, G-d will answer."

I am not a scholar. Instead, I often find myself asking Hashem for an answer to difficult questions. Almost invariably, a little while later, I find the answer I need, and it becomes a part of what I share and what I write.

I don't think this is anything unusual. I believe *all of us* can do this. We just have to be open to asking, and then be ready to listen to the answers we are given.

Joseph Cox lives in Modiin, Israel and is blessed with a wonderful wife and six children. If this book added to your life, do someone else a favor and share it. Also, *please please* add a review online. It makes an enormous difference.

That's me!

Other Books by the Author

Adult Fiction

The City on the Heights (a novel)

Candidate Everyone

The Hidden Agent

The Boulevard, Torah Shorts Volume 2

The Assessors, Torah Shorts Volume 3

Pete and the Felon, Torah Shorts Volume 4

The Barn, Torah Shorts Volume 5

Children's Fiction

Grobar and the Mind Control Potion

Squiggles and the Pit of Destruction

Non-Fiction

A Multi Colored Coat, an Autobiography of Sorts

www.ingramcontent.com/pod-product-compliance
Lightning Source LLC
Chambersburg PA
CBHW020909180626
46816CB00007BA/2325